STOLEN TREASURES AT PICTURED ROCKS

by
Mary Morgan

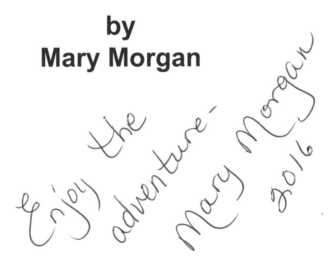

Enjoy the adventure –
Mary Morgan
2016

Illustrated by Dawn McVay Baumer
© Buttonwood Press 2011
978-0-9823351-3-0

Books by Mary Morgan

Published by Buttonwood Press, LLC

Stolen Treasures at Pictured Rocks

© Mary Morgan, 2011

ISBN = 978-0-9823351-3-0

The Face at Mount Rushmore

© Mary Morgan, 2012

ISBN = 978-0-9823351-7-8

Spies in Disguise at Gettysburg

© Mary Morgan, 2013

ISBN = 978-0-9891462-2-7

Disclaimer

Stolen Treasures at Pictured Rocks is a product of
the imagination of the author. None of the events
described in this story occurred. This story has no
purpose other than to entertain and educate the reader.
Names of all characters in the book are used with
permission. Photographs on page 120 are used
with permission by
Pictured Rocks National Lakeshore Park.

Manufactured by Color House Graphics, Inc., Grand Rapids, MI, USA
March 2014
Job #42399

Published by

Buttonwood Press, LLC
P.O. Box 716
Haslett, Michigan 48840
www.buttonwoodpress.com

Chapter 1

"Ben, watch out!" yelled Bekka Cooper, as she watched her normally, not so clumsy, twin brother trip on something sticking up on the beach.

"NO-O-O!" was all Ben could get out as he felt himself falling face first, in slow motion. *What beastly barnacle from a shipwreck washed up on shore and tripped me,* he thought as the sand particles got closer. His arms, flapping like wet noodles, were powerless to stop him. He knew the landing was going to be bad. Ben was convinced he would spend the rest of their vacation at Pictured Rocks with his nose in a cast. And with that, his face landed, sinking two inches down into the biggest, grainiest and hardest sand he had ever seen or felt.

Bending over him, Bekka wasn't sure if she should laugh or call 9-1-1.

"You okay?"

Ben started to move. "This sand is nasty," he said, jumping up, spitting out a mouthful as he brushed off his clothes. He looked around to see if anyone had seen him make a fool of himself on this, the first day of their camping trip. Without saying another word, he headed down the beach in search of treasure that might have drifted ashore from a shipwreck. His goal was to find something really big and make the headline in the Lansing State Journal newspaper, where their father was a reporter. Their mother said he and Bekka inherited a nose for the news, but right now, his nose hurt.

As the soles of their shoes made fresh impressions in the wet sand, they kept in mind the information the park ranger gave them when they registered their camper: "Pictured Rocks National Lakeshore is a very special place in Michigan's Upper Peninsula. It's a forty-mile-long shoreline that is treated like a national park. It's protected by rangers who work to preserve wildlife, natural habitats, and the environment. Just off the shore, are many sunken ships, and sometimes, during storms, pieces wash up on the beach. *Leave them there*. Each ship has its own story, and we want to preserve history and nature. If everyone took something from one of those ships, soon there wouldn't be anything left for visitors to see. Also, don't pick wildflowers, plants, or cut down trees for firewood. We sell firewood in bundles here at the center."

"Wouldn't it be cool if we found a cannon ball or a piece of gold from one of those sunken ships out there?" Ben asked.

His foot pushed around the object he'd found only to discover it was an old brown bottle. Disappointed it wasn't anything special, they walked farther down the beach. The wind seemed to blow harder the longer they walked. Bekka's ponytail blew in the wind, while Ben's cap threatened to blow off into the lake. Both were amazed at how clear the water was. They'd heard Lake Superior is the largest and the coldest of the five Great Lakes, but Ben wanted to test the temperature for himself.

Taking off his tennis shoe, he stuck his big toe into the water as a wave came up on shore. Two seconds later, he jerked it back out.

"C-c-c-cold," was all he could say as he quickly put his shoe back on.

"I'm thinking we'll do more hiking than swimming," replied Bekka, taking his picture with her new camera.

"Hey, I think I see something weird up there," Ben shouted, as he ran farther along the shore.

"Aw, it's just a stick with seaweed wrapped around it," his sister said, as she caught up to him. She used to be as fast a runner as he was, but lately it seemed he could outrun her whenever they raced. Mom said he was in a growing spurt and now his legs were longer and faster, or so it seemed. Just then, something caught her eye. Turning her head to the right she said, "Look at the seagulls! They're circling around that tree up there. I wonder why."

"Let's go look," Ben said, as he started to climb a sand dune. He'd never climbed a dune before, so he didn't realize that, as he took a step upward, he also slipped back down. Grabbing a handful of tall grass, he caught himself and moved upward. Bekka managed to reach the top the same time he did. *Maybe girls are better sand dune climbers than boys,* she thought. Surprising both of them, a wild animal stuck its head out between two bushes. As quickly as it appeared, it scooted out of sight, back into the bushes.

"What was that?" Ben asked.

"I'm not sure, but it had a long tail," Bekka said. "I tried to get a picture of it, but it was too fast for me. Maybe we should head back to the camper, my stomach's growling."

Ben got the feeling Bekka didn't want to be too far from their parents if a wild animal was nearby. Forgetting the seagulls overhead, they turned back toward Lake Superior. Sliding down the sand dune was a lot easier than going up, and soon they were back at the water's edge. For as far as they could see, nothing on the beach looked like part of a ship.

"How far out do you think the sunken ships are?" Ben asked.

"I don't know, but Mom said we're going on a boat tour tomorrow. We can get a good look at the sunken ships then."

They walked along the shore looking for something interesting to take a picture of.

"Stand still and I'll take your picture by that seaweed stick," Bekka said, as they walked by the stick again. "Maybe it's from a two-hundred-year-old tree from that island over there."

In the distance, a freighter sailed east on its way to Lake Michigan or Lake Huron. It looked to be the size of a toy boat, but it was probably longer than a football field.

Ben wondered what it would have been like being a sailor long ago, crossing the waters of the Great Lakes in a storm. He'd heard of the rough waves, cold weather, and dark nights. He was looking forward to tomorrow's boat trip. He wanted to see what lay beneath the surface of the lake. *Binoculars,* he must not forget to take his binoculars.

"Ben! Bekka!" a familiar voice called their names. "There's someone I want you to meet."

Chapter 2

Racing toward their father, Ben and Bekka saw two people with him.

"Ben, Bekka, I'd like you to meet Mr. Hartley and his son, Eli."

Noticing Eli was just about their height, Ben guessed him to be about their age. He had sandy blond hair with freckles on his cheeks.

"Hi," all three said at the same time.

"Eli and his dad are here on a kayaking trip and have a tent right near our camper. We thought you three would have fun together. We invited them to eat dinner with us. How about a hot dog and s'mores in five minutes?"

Ben didn't need any coaxing, so ran ahead to see if the campfire was ready. His stomach was growling.

"Hot dogs are my favorite! I think I can eat three tonight," he announced, as he ran up to their campsite.

"That must have been some hike you took at the beach if you came back that hungry," his mother said, putting the ketchup and mustard on the picnic table.

"Can I have a s'more first?" asked Bekka, as she picked up the package of chocolate bars.

"In your dreams, my dear girl," was all her mom had to say. Bekka loved chocolate and cooking marshmallows on a stick, so putting them together on graham crackers made s'mores one of her all time favorite foods. She couldn't wait 'til she could have one.

"Okay, everyone, grab a stick and put a hot dog on it," Dad said, as he ripped open the package.

While eating with Eli and his dad, Ben's family learned about them. They were from Dimondale, a town near Lansing, and they often canoed on the Grand River. Kayaking sounded like fun, so they decided to try it on Lake Superior, even going into the caves under the cliffs at Pictured Rocks. They had reserved a kayak in Munising.

Mr. Hartley gave some of the history of the area, "Pictured Rocks got its name because the cliff and rocks look like they were painted by an artist for a picture. The sandstone cliffs have several shades of brown and tan and rise two hundred feet above the lake. Believe me, the lakeshore is very protected. Eli learned a good lesson several years ago when he picked his mother a handful of daisies. A ranger saw them on our table and gave us a good warning."

Eli had an embarrassed grin on his face. Ben and Bekka would remember that rule for sure.

Mr. Hartley continued talking, "Behind the lakeshore and the cliffs are several waterfalls, miles of hiking trails, and a famous logging slide at a sand dune."

"A logging slide?" Ben asked.

"Over a hundred years ago, the land above the cliffs was full of pine trees which were cut down for houses and stores. The lumberjacks had to get them to sawmills to cut them into boards. The fastest way was to slide them

11

down the sand dune into the water. Men on rafts would float the logs to a barge, where they would then be taken to the sawmill in Munising. I was planning to take Eli there this week. If you want to, your family could join us."

Turning to his parents, Ben asked, "That sounds awesome, can we go?"

"Sure," replied his father. "We want to see places like that while we are here."

"I will warn you, it's three hundred feet above the lake and can be dangerous for anyone who gets too close to the sliding area. Many, who have fallen over the edge, slid straight down into Lake Superior, and had to be rescued back to safety. I once heard they had to send in Coast Guard helicopters and park rangers in boats just to get to the people."

Three pairs of eyes got even bigger when their imaginations ran wild just thinking about it. Ben and Bekka remembered what it took to climb a dune which was ten feet high. Falling three hundred feet – well, that would make the headline in any newspaper!

"And now, before the fire goes out, we need to get some marshmallows roasting to make our s'mores," said Dad, as Mom opened the bag.

Bekka was the first to shove two plump globs of white sugary goodness onto her skewer. She knelt down close to the campfire's dying embers, turning the marshmallows so they didn't burn. Soon they were a golden brown.

Walking over to the table, she popped one of the marshmallows in her mouth and exhaled a hot breath.

"H-h-hot, but so good." She blew out through her lips. With her fingertips, she took the other marshmallow off the skewer and put it on a graham cracker. Stacking half a chocolate bar on top, and topping it with a second graham cracker, she gave a quick squish and then took her first bite. "Yummy. Just as good as I remembered them."

Ben and Eli didn't wait long to make their s'mores, either. Being boys, they devoured one and moved right back to the fire with more marshmallows on their skewers.

"What a way to end our first day," Ben said after eating two of them. Traces of chocolate and gooey marshmallow lined his lips, but in the darkness, no one could tell. *A guy could learn to like this kind of life*, he thought to himself as he stared into the fire.

"Yes, it's been fun, and now it's time to call it a night," Mr. Hartley said, as he stood up. "Eli and I have a date with a kayak tomorrow morning. There are a couple caves we want to explore. What's your family doing?"

"We're going on a boat tour around Pictured Rocks and up along the lakeshore," Mom replied. "We want to see sunken ships and hear what happened to them. Maybe we'll see you two paddling in or out of the caves as we pass by."

Mom liked to plan each day's events. Ben and
Bekka didn't mind because it was usually adventurous and
never boring. Her motto was, "An active family is a happy
family."

"With that in mind, I think we should pour water on
this fire and-" Dad's voice was hushed by a howling sound
coming from the nearby woods. Goosebumps crept up
everybody's spine.

Chapter 3

"What's that?" questioned Bekka, as she stepped closer to her father. Darkness was coming over them and the orange glow of the campfire was the only light they had. Ben ran for a flashlight.

"My best guess," Dad replied, "is that it's a coyote or a timber wolf. They usually don't bother people, but they howl at the night sounds." His voice was reassuring, so she felt a lot safer. She wondered if it was a wolf or coyote that they saw run off into the bushes that afternoon.

Back with a flashlight, Ben asked, "Do wolves or coyotes have long tails? We saw something with a long tail when we were up on a trail this afternoon."

"It may have been a red fox going to the lake for an afternoon drink," suggested Mr. Hartley. "Can you describe his tail?"

As they tried to remember the coloring of the tail, a man with a flashlight came walking toward their campsite. It was so dark, his light looked almost like a spotlight.

As he got closer, they saw his official-looking hat and realized he was a park ranger. He shone his flashlight around the area, checking for safety violations.

"Good evening, folks. Enjoying your campfire?"

"We sure are," answered Dad. "In fact, we were discussing plans for tomorrow. Our friends are going kayaking under the cliffs, and we're taking a boat tour, and then maybe a hike on one of the trails."

"May I suggest at some point this week you head down the path over there to the Au Sable Lighthouse? It's an easy walk. A guide will give you a tour to the top where you'll have a great view of the lake and sunken ships nearby. Another suggestion is to drive over to Miner's Castle and hike up to the overlook. But before you go anywhere in the park, stop at the Visitor's Center and get three copies of the Junior Ranger books."

Eli's ears perked up. "Junior Ranger books?"

"At each national park, boys and girls can get a booklet with activities to do while there. They learn how to preserve nature for others to enjoy, observe birds and animals, and can work on projects that help them learn about the park. When they finish doing everything, they can take it back to the Visitor's Center, and have a park ranger sign and stamp it with an official stamp. It's a good adventure for them."

"Can we do it?" asked Bekka, turning toward her parents. "I think it would be fun. Can we have our picture taken with a ranger?"

"Oh brother," moaned Ben, looking at Eli. "She likes to have her picture taken with everybody. Last summer, she went up to a perfect stranger-"

At that very moment, the howling started again, stopping Ben in mid-sentence. This time, the noise seemed a lot closer.

"It sounds like a wolf," said the ranger. "I wouldn't be too concerned, as wolves usually leave campsites alone. But there are black bear here in the U.P. Keep all food and garbage contained. Just be on guard, and don't do anything crazy if one comes near."

"This afternoon we saw an animal with a real long tail," Ben said. "Do you know what it could be?"

"Did it look like a house cat?"

"I'm not sure. Is there another animal that looks like a cat?"

"Yes, it's called an American Marten. It has a body the size of a cat, and can swing from tree to tree. It eats all kinds of insects and frogs, but it's fond of red squirrels. We don't see them too often, but they're very entertaining when we do. Keep your eyes open for one and watch what it does," the ranger said. Turning to Bekka he said, "Now, that's a picture you'll want to get."

Looking at their fire one last time before leaving, the ranger added, "Please put your fire completely out. Fire danger is high this time of year, so we have to be careful of every spark." With that last bit of advice, he was gone, shining his light toward the next campsite.

Chapter 4

Morning dawned with a beautiful sunrise. Mr. and Mrs. Cooper woke to the mournful call of loons out on Lake Superior. Chipmunks chattered as they chased each other around the campsite. Ben and Bekka slept while their parents got up. Wanting to get an early start on the day, Dad began to cook the bacon. Knowing how much his family liked it, he put the whole package into the pan.

It didn't take long for the aroma of sizzling bacon to drift into the camper and up Ben's nostrils. Almost instantly, it brought him out of his sleep. Food! He loved food, especially first thing in the morning. Bekka heard Ben's feet hit the floor and got a wiff of the delicious smell of bacon, too. Her dad always cooked it until it was just the way she liked it– extra crispy. She knew she had better get up fast if she wanted any. Ben could finish off a plate of bacon in no time, if no one stopped him.

"Ben, Bekka, wake up," called their mother. "The bacon is done cooking and Dad is about to scramble some eggs. Come and get it."

Both dashed out the door of the camper, making a beeline for the table.

"Bacon and eggs, the best breakfast ever," Ben said, sitting down on the picnic bench.

As they ate, Ben and Bekka talked about the plan for the day with their parents. They had a feeling this was going to be a vacation filled with adventure.

First, they would go into town and take the shipwreck tour. Following that, they would go to the Visitor's Center at the park to get their Junior Ranger books, so they could work on them all week.

They were just about done eating when Eli and Mr. Hartley unzipped their tent and walked toward their own picnic table with a box of cereal and bowls in hand. They were dressed and appeared to be ready to go kayaking.

They could hear Mr. Hartley quizzing Eli on kayak safety and the route they would take once they were in the water.

"We'll leave from Munising, paddle east toward Pictured Rocks, and go under the cliffs at Miner's Castle to check out the caverns and streams."

Eli had had four years of swimming lessons and two years of canoeing with his father, so felt he could handle a kayak safely. They were renting it for four days and planned to explore the whole lakeshore and paddle around nearby Grand Island too.

"Can I go out in your kayak with you this week?" Ben called over to them. He'd never been in a kayak and wanted to try paddling one. Maybe Eli and his father could give him pointers on how to keep from rolling over into the shocking cold water.

"I think that could be arranged," Mr. Hartley offered.

"Cool," he said, jumping up from the table to go get dressed. This was going to be a perfect day.

Thirty minutes later Mom delared, "I think we have everything we need."

She put their lunch and four water bottles in a cooler. Climbing into the car, she set a can of bug spray on the seat beside her. Black flies could be a nuisance, and she wanted to be prepared in case they started biting. Bekka, with her camera strap hanging around her neck, buckled her seatbelt. Just as Dad started to move forward, Ben called out, "Stop the car!"

Chapter 5

"Binoculars! Where did I put my binoculars?" Searching through the camper, Ben found them in the bottom of his backpack, under his goggles and snorkel, which he brought in case they went swimming. "That isn't happening any time soon," he muttered under his breath, as he pulled out the binoculars and darted back out to the car. He could get a better look at the shipwrecks under the surface of the clear water with his binoculars.

His parents could only smile as he climbed back into the car. Usually one of them forgot something and had to go back for it. This time it was Ben.

At the boat dock in Munising, they noticed the parking lot was filled with cars.

"I hope there's room for four more people on the boat," Mom remarked. "Let's hurry and catch it before it leaves."

The sun was bright in a cloudless blue sky. That meant there would be perfect views of the ships below and plenty of stories of the storms that took them down.

"You folks got here just in time," said the ticket-taker at the dock. "Hurry aboard and get your seats. We leave in three minutes."

"Wow," Ben said, taking a window seat. "That was close."

Before long the boat was moving out into the lake, creeping along at a slow speed. So far so good.

As they came to the sites of shipwrecks, everyone leaned over the railings to get a better view. Looking through his binoculars, Ben saw things much closer than those without them. He hoped to see inside the portholes and windows for something valuable. He was fascinated to learn ships like the Michael Groh and Mary M. Scott sunk over one hundred years ago and were still there. Many ships hit the cliffs during storms and sank just off Pictured Rocks' shoreline.

Between shipwrecks, Ben used his binoculars to get a better view of ships in the distance sailing toward faraway ports. Listening to the narrator, he learned that iron ore carriers looked like big barges, and freighters with flags from other countries, passed through to get grain and lumber in other ports. Ben wondered if any of the ships had trouble with pirates.

For two hours they traveled along the coastline. It was amazing to see rock formations shaped like bongo drums, an Indian head, and some with lookouts hanging over the edge.

Bekka was busy taking pictures while Ben used his binoculars. At one point, he saw an eagle soaring overhead and watched it land in a high tree. He was glad he went back for them. One minute later, he spotted kayakers between them and the shore.

"Bekka, I think I see Eli and his dad with a group of other kayakers. Look over there," he said, handing his binoculars to her. She put the strap over her head.

"Wow! It's them," she said, excited to actually be seeing them in their kayak. "They're going into a cave under the cliffs. That would be so much fun. Maybe we can do it sometime."

As she looked through the binoculars, Ben looked up at the overlook on the cliff and spotted someone who looked like they were having a problem.

"Bekka, let me have my binoculars. Quick! Some-one's doing something weird up there."

She whipped the strap back from around her neck and gave them back. Ben watched the action carefully.

At that very moment, a splash was heard on the other side of the tour boat, causing a big commotion.

"Man overboard!"

"Someone throw him a life preserver!"

Bekka and almost everyone else ran over to see what had happened. Several people tried to reach out to the man, but he was way beyond their grasp. Someone ran for a life preserver, while another person grabbed for a life-saving pole. The man kept yelling for someone to save him.

Ben didn't move. He kept his binoculars aimed at the man on the cliff's overlook. Something was suspicious. The man wasn't in trouble. He was signaling someone using flags. Since there were no other boats nearby, the signals had to be for someone on their boat!

Ben knew messages could be sent using semaphore, hand-held flags. They were squares divided into triangles. Each letter of the alphabet had a different movement. His father had been a boy scout and learned the alphabet and movements for a merit badge. Since Ben was a cub scout, his dad taught him the semaphore alphabet, and together, they practiced saying things to each other. Two years ago, he took his dad to school for Show and Tell, surprising even his teacher. His friends were amazed when his father spelled out the message, *"I am Ben's dad."* It was a proud day.

Watching the man on the overlook, Ben thought the guy spelled out the words *meet me tonight.* Just then the tour boat lurched, and turned.

What did that message mean, and who was it meant for, Ben thought to himself. Just then Bekka came running over to him.

"Ben, you missed it! A man fell into the lake and had to be rescued before he froze to death! The boat captain threw him a life-preserver, so he wouldn't drown. I got a picture of him in the water, and then of him being pulled out. He's lucky to be alive!"

"Wow! Where is he? Let me see!"

The man was wrapped in a blanket inside the captain's cabin, trying to get warm. Another man was talking to him, with excitement in his voice, pacing back and forth in the cabin.

Ben leaned toward the window to get a better look and overheard some of what they were saying.

"Yes, I got the message," the pacing man told the man in the blanket. "Falling in the lake was the perfect decoy. I don't think anyone saw Tom up on the ledge."

Just then the man looked up and saw Ben looking at them.

"Get out of here, kid. Mind your own business," he snarled.

Ben jumped back, surprised he had been caught snooping at them. *What did these two men have to do with Tom, the man up on the ledge?* he wondered. Something just wasn't right. He smelled a mystery in the air. He and Bekka would have to do a little investigating. He could see the headlines in the newspaper already, "Reporter's Kids Catch Crooks In The Act". But first, there was something he needed - proof of who was involved. Being a reporter's son was coming in handy.

Chapter 6

Every good story should be backed up by a picture. Turning back around toward the boat's railing, he quietly signaled his sister to get closer to him and then talked almost under his breath.

"Bekka, you took a picture of the guy in the water, right?"

"Yeah, why?"

"Shhh! I need you to do me a favor and fast."

"What?"

"Without letting anyone see you, put your camera up to the window and take a picture of those two guys. Ok?"

"Why?"

"I can't explain right now. Can you just do it?" Ben said, trying not to get annoyed with her. She really was a good sister, but her *thousand* questions could get rather annoying sometimes.

"Do you think they'll get mad?"

"Don't worry about it, just take the picture!" Now he was annoyed.

Bekka slowly lifted her digital camera, snapped a picture and pulled the camera back down quickly. But she didn't move fast enough. The flash caught the men's attention. The man who had growled at Ben lunged toward the door.

Seeing Ben, he yelled, "I thought I told you to mind your own business. Get away from us. NOW!"

His loud voice caused many passengers to look in their direction. Ben and Bekka practically jumped overboard in their haste to get away from the cabin door. The boat captain came around the bow of the boat just in time to see the twins running the length of the boat in search of their parents.

"What happened to you two?" asked their mother when she saw the look of terror on their faces.

"We were taking a picture of the man who fell overboard when his friend yelled at us," Bekka confessed.

"I think you two had better just stay by us for the rest of the cruise. Have you even heard much of what the narrator has been saying?"

"Some," Ben replied, "but I think something big is happening, and I bet those two guys in the captain's cabin are involved."

"What do you mean by that?" Bekka asked. Her eyes suddenly got bigger. She thought she was just taking a picture of the two men. "You almost got us into trouble."

"Did your *nose for the news* start sniffing again?" their mother asked him.

Ben looked around to be sure no one was watching or listening before he began his story.

"When the guy fell into the lake, I think he did it on purpose to distract anyone from seeing what was going on up at the cliff." The more he talked, the more excited his voice got.

"I was watching Eli and his dad kayaking through my binoculars, when I spotted a guy up on the lookout with flags in his hands. He started sending semaphore signals, spelling out words." His hands started doing motions.

"What was he signaling?" asked their dad when he heard semaphore signals were involved.

"Meet me tonight."

"Meet me tonight?" questioned his sister.

"Yes, meet me tonight."

"It makes you wonder why someone would risk his life jumping into a freezing cold lake just so no one would see someone up on the ledge. Why couldn't they just use their cell phones?" Bekka asked.

"Yeah. That guy who jumped in the lake was crazy if you ask me. I could only put my toe in for a second," declared Ben. He turned toward the shoreline again, putting his binoculars back up to his eyes to see if he could spot the man on the cliff again.

Instead of seeing the stranger again, he saw something that made him take a double look.

More suspicious action.

Chapter 7

The tour boat was about to go beyond the rocky cliff area where a stream fed into Lake Superior. The narrator mentioned there were waterfalls several miles away which flowed down the stream, and ended up at Lake Superior near the overlook. Years ago in that very spot, a number of ships hit the rocks during storms, and sank. The water was crystal clear, so canoers and kayakers had a good view of things down below.

Looking toward the shore through his binoculars, Ben thought he saw someone get out of a canoe, reach down into the water and then put something into the canoe. The person looked in the direction of the tour boat, climbed back into the canoe, and paddled quickly up the stream beside the cliff walls, out of sight.

"Bekka, quick, take a picture of that canoe."

"What canoe?" She aimed her camera and clicked.

"Mom," Ben said excitedly, "I think I just saw someone take something out of the water and put it into his canoe. I think he stole something from a shipwreck."

"What did it look like?"

"I couldn't tell, but it wasn't very big."

"Did you get a look at the person's face in your binoculars?"

"No, he was too far away, but I could tell the canoe was painted camouflage colors."

Mom frowned. "Remember the ranger said no one can take anything out of the water? That guy is breaking the park rules. It makes you wonder what's so valuable for him to risk getting caught."

As the canoe disappeared up the stream along the cliffs, the tour boat narrator pointed out Miner's Castle.

"Miner's Castle!" Ben exclaimed, "that's where Eli and his dad were going. We'll have to ask them if they saw a camouflage canoe pass them today."

Two freaky things happening in one day. What was going on? During the rest of the boat ride, Ben kept his binoculars glued to the shoreline and cliffs while Bekka kept her camera ready to snap a picture. There was definitely something suspicious happening around Pictured Rocks, and they were the eye witnesses.

Chapter 8

After they returned to the dock in Munising, Ben and Bekka couldn't wait to get to Pictured Rocks Visitor's Center at Sand Point to report what they had witnessed. Ranger Greg frowned as he listened to their story.

"People stealing maritime artifacts is the biggest problem we have in the park."

"Maritime what?" asked Ben.

"Maritime artifacts. They're items which come ashore from sunken ships, mainly after storms, like door knobs, brass portholes, lengths of chain, and sometimes even anchors."

"Wow," Bekka exclaimed. "Do they just lie on the beach?"

"Yes, until sand buries them, or a storm takes them back out into the water, or someone steals them," he said, with concern in his voice. "Why do you think it's important to leave things alone when you see them on the beach?"

"Because if everyone took something, before long there wouldn't be anything left for other people to look at," she answered, repeating what she heard yesterday.

"Exactly. That's why we count on people like you to do the right thing by not picking up any maritime artifacts, and reporting someone who does. Sometimes we are able to catch people with items in their cars before they leave the park, and then they are in big trouble."

Ben's eyebrows shot up. "Really?"

"Yes. Anyone caught with stolen goods has to pay a very big fine. We have a museum at the end of the National Shoreline in Grand Marais, filled with displays from shipwrecks. Some are the things we took out of people's cars and campers."

As he talked, Ben and Bekka's eyes got bigger just thinking of being in that much trouble. There was no way they were going to pick up anything from a shipwreck.

"Now, let's make the rest of your visit in the park a good one." Turning toward their parents, Ranger Greg gave them brochures and maps with ideas for day hikes to waterfalls and beaches along the lakeshore. He then gave Ben and Bekka Junior Ranger booklets filled with assignments to work on. They looked at pictures of birds, trees, waterfalls, animal tracks, and other things they needed to identify. It was going to make their time at Pictured Rocks very interesting.

"I hope you complete the books before you leave," Ranger Greg said to the twins. "You'll learn the history of our park, see how Indians used to catch fish, discover what birds and animals call this their home, and hike around a few trails. I hope you have good hiking shoes," he said, looking down at their feet.

Both were glad they had on their tennis shoes, because every trail they saw on the map had a long path and lots of steps to climb.

The ranger continued with information. "There is one word that best describes our park. It has to do with the many people that have lived here, all the industries that were here, sites to see, and animals that live in it. It starts with the letter D. It's mentioned in your books, but that is the only hint I'll give you. When you finish the books, bring them back, and I'll give you something special."

"Cool," said Ben, looking at his copy.

"Oh yes, one last thing," the ranger added. "If you happen to be on a beach and you see a striped bird with orange legs, have fun watching it run with a stop-and-start movement. It is the Piping Plover and is considered an endangered species. They run along, calling out with a shrill bell or whistle sound. There used to be hundreds of them along Lake Superior, but now there are only twenty pairs left. You might see their nests in the sand and grass by the shore. Please don't go near them."

Ben closed his book. "Can we have another one? We have a friend who is out kayaking with his dad, and he can do it with us."

"Sure. It's a great way for every Junior Ranger to learn more about our park and how to preserve it."

Turning toward Mr. Cooper, the ranger said, "I suggest you go to Hurricane River Campground and take the trail out to the Au Sable Lighthouse Station."

"Hurricane River," Ben interrupted, "that's where we're camping."

"Great, then it will be easy for you to find."

"How long a hike is it to the lighthouse?" asked Dad.

"It's about a mile-and-a-half walk. You will have woods on one side and underbrush on the other, but there are lots of places where you can look through and see Lake Superior. If you time it right, you might see families of loons swimming nearby looking for a fish dinner. Did you know they can stay under water for five minutes diving for fish? They have razor sharp beaks, so don't mess with them."

Loons, thought Bekka. *I just saw a picture of a loon in my Junior Ranger book. If we see one, I'm going to take a picture and show my friends. There aren't any loons in Lansing.*

Ranger Greg kept talking. "You can take a tour of the lighthouse and the home where the lightkeeper's family lived. The lighthouse was built in 1874 and has helped guide many ships around the tricky waters in the harbor ever since. If it wasn't for the lighthouse, many more ships would be laying underwater in Lake Superior."

Just then, Mom came over with a stack of brochures in her hand. "I have enough ideas here to last us all week. Let's look at them while we eat our picnic lunch and decide what to do first." Thanking the ranger for his help, they all headed outside.

Munching on their sandwiches at an outdoor table near the Visitor's Center, Bekka discovered they could walk behind waterfalls, and Ben looked on a map for the cliff overlook where they saw the guy making hand signals. Dad thought the Log Slide looked interesting, while Mom looked at the variety of wildflowers growing everywhere.

Picking up her Junior Ranger book, Bekka said, "Ben, let's make this a scavenger hunt and see if we can do them all." Turning a page in the book, she noticed a warning about leaving big fishing nets in the water.

"Oh no, look what it says can happen to loons when they dive underwater for fish." She closed her eyes fast.

Chapter 9

The books instructed them to identify trees growing in the forests, so a hike seemed the natural thing to do. They all agreed to head for the trail to Miner's Falls.

"Dad, is it near the lookout at Miner's Castle?" Ben asked, wanting to see the overlook where the man had sent the semaphore signals.

Looking at a map, Dad said, "Well, it looks like we could walk to the falls, and then drive on to the overlook."

"Then let's go," Ben said, eager to get there.

Walking along the trail, they made notes in their books of the trees and birds they saw. Everyone was glad for the shoes they had chosen to wear, especially on the steps leading to the platform overlooking the falls. Some were wet and slimy from the mist in the air. They could hear the rush of water falling over rocks and knew they weren't far from the falls.

"How many steps do you think there are?" asked Mom, looking straight ahead.

"One hundred," guessed Bekka. "I'm going to count them and see how close I was."

Ben took off on a trot, hanging onto the handrail. He knew if he didn't, he'd hear one of his parents telling him to be careful. A small stream ran along some of the steps. A salamander perched himself on top of a twig. He stopped to look at it. *You probably think you are camouflaged and I can't see you, kind of like the canoe I saw,* he thought. If he had a good place to keep it, it might make a fun pet. As if the salamander could read Ben's mind, he dashed away under a bush. Ben kept going and beat everyone to the falls overlook.

"Seventy-seven," he heard Bekka call out, as she stepped onto the platform and went right to the railing.

"Wow! Look at the waterfalls," she exclaimed. "Can somebody get my picture? I want to show this to Hannah when I get home." Her friend, Hannah, took pictures on vacations and showed them to Bekka all the time.

"Wait a minute. Are these the waterfalls you can walk behind?" she asked. "I want my picture taken with water falling all over me."

"No, these aren't the ones," Mom informed her, "but why don't both of you get in the picture?"

Ben preferred to sit on the rail while his sister just stood by it. She had no desire to fall fifty feet backwards into the water below. Mom held her breath while taking the picture. Visions of Ben flipping backward were more than she could think about.

"Okay, seventy-seven steps down means seventy-seven steps up. And then, a mile hike back to our car," a voice behind them said. Turning to see who was talking, Ben saw two ladies who looked old enough to be grandmothers smiling at him.

"Hi there," one of them said. "Where are you from?"

"Lansing."

"That's nice. What's it like to live in the capital city?"

"It's okay. There's lots more people and places to go than there are up here. Where do you live?"

"We live in Newberry, not far away. I come to Pictured Rocks each summer and visit where I grew up. My grandfather and father were the lighthouse keepers at Au Sable Point so we walk out to visit my old house."

"You lived at the lighthouse?" Ben asked, hardly believing he was meeting someone who really grew up at a lighthouse.

"Yes, it was very lonely and cold, particularly in the winter time. For many years, there wasn't a road out to it. You could only get to it by boat and then you needed to climb up the sand dune hill it is built on."

Bekka couldn't help overhearing them, so joined in on the conversation. "Did you like living there?"

"I had two brothers, and sometimes we were able to have friends stay overnight with us. My father would always have the lights on to help guide the ships safely into the harbor. They used to use kerosene, but now they have electricity and solar panels. Plus, the lights are on timers, making it easier for everyone. Ships still need the lights so they don't crash into the rocks."

"Did you ever see a ship crash and sink?" Ben asked, always wanting to hear dramatic stories.

"Well, yes, and no. We had many storms that seemed to toss ships around and sometimes they came dangerously close to the rocks near Au Sable Point, but I didn't actually see one sink. My grandfather saw several go down. They didn't have the sturdy built ships like we do today. Did you ever hear about the Edmund Fitzgerald sinking?"

"No."

"Well, it was a large ship that sank in a bad storm on Lake Superior in November of 1975. I remember it like it was yesterday. News about it spread all over our country and a song was written about it. The bell and other

artifacts are in the museum at Whitefish Point over near the Sault Sainte Marie Locks. People up here call them the Soo Locks. Have you ever been there?"

"No."

"It's got lots of interesting things from ships that you might like to see and you would hear stories about storms on the Great Lakes. Your family will have to go there someday if you like old ships. For sure, you'll have to visit my lighthouse. We'll go there tomorrow. One hike a day is enough for us."

"Hey, dad, this lady used to live at the lighthouse and she's going there tomorrow. Can we hike there, too?"

"I think it's a great idea. Who knows, maybe we'll see you ladies there." Turning to Ben and Bekka, he said, "I think it's time for us to head back to our campsite and see if Eli and his dad had as much adventure as we did."

Chapter 10

That night, while their mother wrote postcards in the camper, the twins, Eli, and their fathers sat around the fire pit on the beach where the Hurricane River flowed into Lake Superior. They told stories of their day. Eli begged to go first.

"Before we left the dock, a man measured me and my dad, and gave us a kayak that fit us. We had to wear a life vest in case we rolled over and fell out. The man made us practice paddling in the shallow water, and we did okay. We never tipped over, even once."

"I think canoeing back home on the Grand River helped us learn how to keep our balance in a kayak and not flip over," his father added, nodding his head.

"Did you go to the shipwrecks?" asked Ben.

"Yeah, it was so cool. We could see the decks and other parts right up close," Eli replied.

"We did too. I had my binoculars and could see way down too."

"I took lots of pictures," Bekka cut in. "Ben saw you in his binoculars, so I got one of your kayak when we passed you. I can't wait to have my pictures printed."

"You'll have to make a copy for us too," Mr. Hartley said. "We need one to prove we really did it. Eli has an uncle who was sure we'd flip over first thing."

"How far do you think you paddled?" asked Ben.

"Well, let's see, how many miles did we figure we went today, Eli? Was it six or seven?"

Rubbing his still sore arms, Eil said, "My sore muscles think we went six or seven *hundred* miles."

"We rented our kayak for three more days, would you two like to try it down here at the beach tomorrow?"

"Yeah," Ben and Bekka said together. Their voices were so similar, it sounded like only one of them answered.

"Good. Since you both are about Eli's size, you can use his life jacket. How long do you think you can hold your breath should we roll over and go under the water?"

"Not very long," replied Ben. "Can I wear nose plugs?"

"Sure, if you want to. Just remember, that water is very cold. You won't want to be in it very long. Now, how was your day?"

Chapter 11

Bekka opened her mouth, but Ben spoke first. "Awesome."

"No, scary," she said. "A man fell off our boat."

"No way!" exclaimed Eli.

"Yeah, a guy up on a cliff did a semaphore message to a man on our boat. It was his friend who fell in," Bekka explained, her tongue almost tripping on her words.

"And then we got yelled at by the man because we took his picture," Ben added. Eli couldn't believe it.

"And Ben saw somebody get out of his canoe and take something out of the water and put it in his canoe, and then the man paddled up a stream really fast so no one could get a good look at him," Bekka continued, excitedly.

"We told the ranger about it, and he'll be watching for a camouflage canoe," Ben said, ending their story.

"Wow, you did have excitement on your boat. When you saw the man doing signals, could any of you understand what he was trying to say?" asked Mr. Hartley.

"Yes," Ben said. "He signaled, meet me tonight."

"Wow, how could you tell?"

"My dad taught me," Ben replied, looking at his dad.

"When I was a boy scout, I learned semaphore signals using flags, and since Ben will need to know them for a merit badge someday, I taught him the alphabet a couple years ago. It's impressive he remembered it enough to decipher the message."

"I'm impressed too," Mr. Hartley said in return. He stretched out his legs and put his hands behind his head, as he looked out across Lake Superior. "Do any of you know what the Indians used to call this lake?"

"No," replied three young voices.

"Gitchee Gumee. Any idea what it means?"

"No," responded three young voices again.

"It means Big Water. A poet by the name of Henry Wadsworth Longfellow wrote a poem called *The Song of Hiawatha.* It begins, "By the shores of Gitchee Gumee, By the shining Big-Sea-Water". And that's all I remember. Now that I have seen the Big Sea Water, I'll have to find the poem and read it again. Apparently, there was a lot more wildlife than there is now. Imagine looking over there and seeing a moose coming down to drink. Imagine being in a canoe and paddling all the way across. I wonder how many miles it is to the other shore. Did you know you would be in Canada?"

The ten-year-olds strained their eyes and couldn't see the other side. Mr. Hartley's information was very interesting and time flew by.

Hearing a mournful call, Bekka exclaimed, "Hey, there's a family of loons out there. Five  babies with an adult in front and one in the back. The ranger said they go fishing for food at this time of the day."

"Eli, look, one of the big ones just went underwater. The ranger told us it could stay under for five minutes," Ben informed him.

"Wow." Eli was amazed it was underwater so long. "I wonder how deep it has to go to get a fish?"

Just then the loon bobbed back up and looked like he was swallowing a fish in his neck.

"Wait a minute! I wanted to get a picture of a loon. I need my camera." Bekka turned it on and aimed in the loons' direction. Getting a picture of all seven loons wasn't easy, since one or two kept bobbing up and down into the water, looking for a fish.

"There must be a lot of fish out there," Dad said. "It'll be hard getting them all in the picture. You might end up with the tail feathers of one rather than its head."

"Got it," Bekka said, clenching her fist like a champ. She finally caught all seven above the surface at one time.

As they finished telling their stories, the fire died out. The sun set, casting a final red glow over the lake.

Darkness fell. A peaceful feeling came over them and no one moved. The gentle lapping of water onto the shore was the only sound they heard.

Suddenly, in the dim light of the rising moon, they saw, and then heard, movement in the water. A canoe was in the lake, moving ever so quietly. And then it happened, taking everyone by surprise.

Chapter 12

Someone snapped a flashlight on and off farther down the beach. It looked like a signal to someone in the canoe. Someone in the canoe then flicked their flashlight on and off. And then, they heard a splash.

Someone was out in the lake after dark.

What was going on?

Ben cupped his hands to his mouth to yell out to them, but his father laid his hand on his arm.

"Shhh. I think they're up to no good. That water is too cold for an evening swim. Let's just watch what happens and listen to their conversation."

Bekka wasn't too sure she wanted to be there.

"Do you think someone is stealing stuff from ships, Dad? Maybe this is how crooks do it, after dark."

"I'm not sure," he whispered. "That's why we're listening for now. We can't see very well and we don't know how many are on the shore down there. They must have walked down the trail toward the lighthouse and cut through the bushes to the water. I wonder if they're camping near us."

After several minutes of hearing things being put into the canoe, Mr. Hartley and Mr. Cooper came up with a plan. If something criminal was happening, they had to stop it before more valuable artifacts were stolen. The three kids would stay by the firepit while the men walked down the beach to surprise the would-be crooks in the act.

"Shouldn't you call 9-1-1?" asked Bekka. "I think this is a robbery. Do you want me to scream and scare them off?" Her screams could send anyone running.

"No. In case a robbery isn't going on, we shouldn't call 9-1-1. We'll just walk down and surprise them," Mr. Hartley decided. "I don't think anyone would hurt us, and if it appears suspicious, we'll report it to the ranger tomorrow."

"Okay, let's go," Mr. Cooper said. "You three stay here. We'll be right back."

"Be careful, Dad," Bekka cautioned.

"We will."

And with that, the two men walked down the beach. Eli, Ben, and Bekka felt very much alone in the dark by the shore of the largest Great Lake. Someone was in the canoe, someone was in the water and someone was on the shore. What was going on? What would happen to their fathers? They could just barely make out their fathers' forms walking silently on the beach. Suddenly, the man in the water surfaced. He had a diver's headlamp and as he looked toward shore, the light shone right on the two dads.

"Someone's coming! Get out of here!" the man in the water yelled, and swam back over to the canoe. Just then the man on shore shone his light in the faces of the two dads, blinding them.

The man on the beach took off running farther up the shore and then cut into the bushes. Not having flashlights, the dads couldn't pursue him.

Mr. Hartley yelled, "Stop! We're going to report this!"

The three kids huddled together as they heard loud voices shouting in the dark distance. Would their fathers come back safely, or would something happen to them? Just then, a small white light flickered in the dark water. The men in the canoe must have needed a light to keep from crashing into the dangerous rocks off shore. They were getting away, but where was the guy who was on shore?

They didn't wonder long. Behind them, they heard a rustling noise on the path which led to the campsite. Not knowing the three were sitting on the beach watching, the man shone his light for just a second on the path ahead of him. As quickly as it came on, it went back off. Everything happened so fast. And it was so very dark.

"I'm scared," Bekka whimpered.

"Shhh!" her brother whispered in her ear. "We don't want him to know we are here."

She couldn't help herself,
"D-A-A-D!"

A bloodcurdling scream erupted out of her mouth and the three of them froze. Now, everyone knew they were there.

Chapter 13

"I'm coming!" her dad called, running as fast as he could, realizing a stranger was possibly headed for the three kids.

Totally out of breath, he knelt down by Bekka and held her. She threw her arms around him in an instant.

"The man with the flashlight ran right back there and it scared me," she whimpered. She almost let out another cry, but she pushed it back down inside.

"That means he could be camping here too. There are ten campsites in this section, so he might be nearby. Something is going on, and it's a little too close for comfort. Let's go back to the camper and come up with a plan to keep us safe. I don't think anyone could recognize us out there in the dark."

With that, they were off to the camper to tell their mother what had happened and exchange cell phone numbers with Eli's dad, in case they had to get ahold of each other in a hurry.

One look at their faces told Mom something was up.

"What happened? You all look like you saw a ghost."

"Not exactly, but close," her husband replied.

"Seriously?"

"We were sitting quietly by the lake watching loons go by before the sun set. All of a sudden, after it got kind of dark, a canoe came out of nowhere. Somebody jumped out of it into the water, and someone on the shore shined his light." Ben's words were just flying out of his mouth. His mother's eyes got two sizes larger and her jaw dropped.

Eli added, "Then our dads decided to walk down and surprise them. But the man in the water came up with a light on his head still shining, and he saw them on the beach. He must have gotten back into the canoe, and the man on the beach ran away into the bushes, and then he ran behind us on the path and Bekka screamed and…"

"You men left the three kids all alone on the beach?" she said, raising her voice. Her hands went instantly to her hips as her head jerked toward her husband.

"They could have been hurt!"

"Mom, we're okay," Ben said bravely. "Bekka just got scared. She didn't need to scream. She's such a girl."

"I did too need to scream," Bekka retorted, wanting to defend herself.

"Okay, that's enough. I think we have had enough excitement for one day," Mom stated. "Tomorrow we'll have a quieter day, taking a hike to the lighthouse and exploring the beach. If anyone is up to something, I don't want us anywhere near it. If there's a crime happening, let the rangers deal with it. Our family does not need to make headline news here in the Munising newspaper. We're on vacation!"

From the tone of her voice, Ben and Bekka knew she meant business, so they didn't say a word.

Mr. Hartley and Eli agreed that a day of kayaking at the beach and hiking to the lighthouse would be a great plan and turned to leave the camper.

As Eli's hand was about to open the door, they heard a snapping sound on the back side of the camper under the window near where they had been talking. Someone had been listening to them.

Bekka buried her head in a pillow so she wouldn't scream! She just couldn't help it.

Chapter 14

Eli, stay here," Mr. Hartley said, as he and Mr. Cooper bounded outside, flashlights in hand. After searching for ten minutes, shining their lights in all directions, the men returned to the camper.

"Did you see anyone, Dad?" asked Bekka.

"No. Whoever was there got away before we could spot him, but the long branch which was lying behind the camper has been stepped on and broken. I think someone was watching us and listening to our story. He might have watched us come up from the beach and came over to the camper. I think we need to meet with Ranger Greg again. What have we gotten ourselves into?" A look of dismay clouded his face.

"Nate, I think you and Eli should stay in the camper with us tonight," Dad suggested.

"Thanks for the offer, Dan, but I think we'll be all right in our tent. I don't think anyone wants to hurt us." Trying to reassure the children, he said, "Maybe it was just a fat raccoon snooping for food under the camper. We'll keep our flashlight and cell phone right by us and we'll see you in the morning." With that, they were off into the darkness, making a stop at the restroom across the parking lot.

"I think we should pull the curtains shut and play a game of Scattergories. Girls against the boys," Mom announced, as she moved toward the window, "and I think we need some popcorn to eat. Sound good?"

"Sounds good to me," Dad said, pulling the game out of the cupboard over the stove. "This has been quite the day, and I prefer it to end in a quiet way. Ben, are you smarter than a fifth grader?"

"Dad, I am a fifth grader!"

"Well, I was just checking, because I want to beat your mother and sister in this game. You roll the dice and we'll see if it's a good letter for us."

"S," Mom said after the dice stopped moving. "Okay, everybody, we have to think of words that answer the questions using the letter 's' as the first letter."

Cracking up, Ben looked at the first question- "Name of a famous lake." That one was easy.

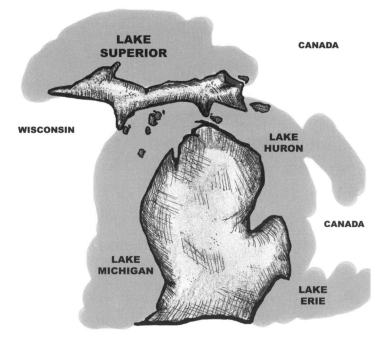

Chapter 15

Bekka rolled over and squinted as the morning sun peeked through the window near her bed. No one else seemed to be awake. Chipmunks squeaked as they chased each other around the picnic table. She lay back and thought of yesterday's excitement. She and Ben just might have to become detectives and figure out what was going on. Suddenly she bolted up on her bed. *Meet me tonight.*   Could it be that the man on the cliff and the men in the canoe and the man on the shore were the ones they saw yesterday while on the boat?

Her heart started racing. Did the men on the beach plan to do something bad? Did Eli and her dad stop them in the act? Were they in danger? Ben had to wake up and hear her suspicions. Now!

"Ben! Ben!" She whispered so loudly, she thought she would wake their parents. He had to help her think this through.

If the men were bad guys, then she had a picture of the one in the water and another picture of the two men in the captain's cabin. This was getting a little scary.

"Ben, you have to wake up," she said with a bit more volume. She threw her pillow, hoping it would wake him.

"Hey," he whined, coming out of a deep sleep. He liked sleeping in, not having a pillow land in his face.

"I just thought of something. Remember what the man's message was?"

"Yeah, *meet me tonight*." His voice went from a whisper to almost a full yell. *"Meet me tonight!"*

"What are you two kids so excited about?" their mother asked from her bed.

"I just thought of something! Remember the guy's message from up on the cliff- *meet me tonight*? Do you think it was him and the guys on our boat who met last night on the beach? Maybe dad and Eli's dad stopped them from doing something illegal."

"Bekka, are you letting your imagination run away from you?"

"No, Mom! Don't you see? It all fits. They're probably camping here too."

Just then Ben and Bekka had the same thought! *It was probably one of the men by their camper last night, not a raccoon.* They were sure it had to be the men from the boat and the man up on the ledge sending signals.

"We have to tell Eli," Ben said, climbing out of his sleeping bag. "Come on Bekka, get dressed. We have to warn him and his dad."

Bekka grabbed her clothes, and in no time they were ready to dash out the door. Mom rolled back over.

"If they aren't awake yet, don't wake them up!"

Chapter 16

Passing by the picnic table, Ben and Bekka stopped dead in their tracks. They were right. They had been spied upon.

Neither one wanted to touch it, but their curiosity was too strong to resist. Skewered onto the end of a stick on the table was a note with big letters:

MIND YOUR OWN BUSINESS!

"Mind your own business," Bekka read. "That's what that man yelled at us yesterday. They know where we are!" She couldn't help herself, she let out another blood curdling scream, "D-A-A-D!"

The door to the camper flew open, as did the zipped flap on the Hartley's tent.

"What's wrong?" called Dad. Picking up the stick, Ben ran to the camper as fast as he could. Eli dashed over to read it too.

"Okay, that does it," Dad said. "We're getting the ranger involved in this. They might be trying to scare us out of here, or they might just be giving us a real warning." He looked at the kids. He was so serious, his eyebrows almost went together.

"Should we go home?" Mom asked.

"No, but I think we will inform the ranger of all that happened last night. We know there was an eavesdropper listening to us talk and now here is this note. We've gotten ourselves in the middle of something, but once we turn it over to the rangers, we'll go on with our vacation. No more nose for the news."

Mr. Hartley seemed to agree they should stay at Pictured Rocks. "We can walk the trail to the lighthouse and then spend time at the beach with the kayak. That seems harmless enough. But first, I agree, we should go to the Visitor's Center and report what happened last night."

"Good idea," Dad said, shaking his head. "Who would have thought our quiet vacation at Hurricane River Campground would turn into something like this? The website said it was peaceful and quiet. Yeah, right."

"Can we go down to the beach and see if we can see anything laying there?" Eli asked his father.

"I'll say *yes* if you three stay together. Yell if you see anyone doing anything suspicious. Promise?"

"We will," Eli called over his shoulder, as they took off to locate the spot where the man had stood with the flashlight last night.

Maybe in the daylight they could see something that had been tampered with.

"Breakfast in ten," Mom yelled after them. With all the excitement, no one remembered they hadn't eaten.

The shoreline looked undisturbed as far as they could see. They were kind of disappointed. Catching thieves appealed to them. Plus they wanted to see something that those men were putting in their canoe. Ben searched high and low. Bekka stopped to look at shells and stones.

"Wow, I just found a Petoskey stone!"

"You did?" Ben stopped looking and went over to see it.

"Sweet," she said, showing it to the boys. "I always wanted to find one. Our teacher said these are fossils and are found only along shores in Michigan." Wetting it in the water, she added, "Look, you can really see the six-sided shapes on it now. Eli, did you ever see one?"

"Yes, my dad has one. He found it when we went camping at Traverse City. He said they are named after the Indian chief, Petoskey, and they named the city of Petoskey after him, too. My dad says they are

Michigan's State stone. He knows a lot of that kind of stuff. I have a collection of shells from when we went to the ocean, but I don't have a Petoskey stone. Maybe I can find one too."

Wanting to help him have his wish, Bekka walked along the shore looking closely at the stones.

"Eli," his father's voice called to him, "you three need to come and eat. We have a big day ahead of us."

They took off running along the beach, racing as they went. Looking for Petoskey stones, once again they'd forgotten they hadn't had breakfast.

When they arrived at the campsite, Mom looked up from reading one of the Junior Ranger books.

"There's a few projects in here you can do today at the beach and when we walk out to the lighthouse. You'll know a great deal about Pictured Rocks when we leave."

"Blueberry pancakes coming right up," announced Dad, flipping several onto a platter. "These aren't just any old blueberries, they are the ones the U.P. is famous for. I tried some. They are dee-licious." His blue lips proved it.

Eli didn't waste any time sitting down at the picnic table. "Thanks for letting us eat with you."

"No problem," Mom said in return. "We have plenty and I'm sure you won't eat us out of house and home. Your dad said tonight he'll make a Hartley specialty meal called hobo dinners."

"Hobo dinners! I love hobo dinners! They're so cool. I can't wait to show you how to do it," said Eli, more than just a little excited. He dove his fork into a stack of three pancakes, squirting blueberry juice into the air.

"Oops, sorry" he said, making a face.

"It's okay, could happen to any of us," Dad assured him, passing the platter to Ben, who dove into them too.

Chapter 17

Ranger Greg was behind the counter at the Visitor's Center when they entered an hour later. He finished answering a camper's question and looked up after folding a map.

"Good morning, folks. I hope you had a great time at the falls yesterday. We haven't heard any more reports concerning someone in a camouflage canoe."

Before he could continue, Dad spoke up. "Well, that's why we're here. We had an incident last evening which we feel you should know about."

"Oh, really? What happened?"

"We were down at the beach at the Hurricane River Campground about eight-thirty watching the sunset and enjoying a fire. After dark, our fire went out, and we sat there listening to the water lap up on shore. All of a sudden, we saw a flashlight flicker on and off from a canoe. Someone farther down the beach from us flashed a light back, and we heard someone splash into the water as they got out of the canoe."

"What did you do?" asked Ranger Greg.

"Nate and I walked down quietly to surprise them, but they saw us and got away. We couldn't tell where the canoe went, but the man on shore ran down the trail toward the campground. We think he is camped near us, because this morning, he left a note on our table telling us to mind our own business."

Everyone watched the ranger's reaction.

"This is not good. I want you to tell your story to my supervisor." Ranger Greg came around to the front of the counter and led them into a private office.

"Sir," Ranger Greg said to his supervisor, "this is Dan and Amy Cooper and their children, and this is Nate Hartley and his son. They have some experiences they would like to report."

Ben, Bekka, and Eli thought it was just too cool to be in the middle of a crime scene – like being in a TV show. They were going to have quite a story to tell their friends back home.

The supervisor listened, rubbing his forehead as he did. He didn't like what he heard. He was very protective of maritime artifacts and wanted to catch someone red-handed if he was stealing them.

"I'm sorry you folks have to be involved, but do keep your eyes and ears open and keep in touch. We'll do the same."

"We hope to have a quiet vacation from here on," Dad said. "It's off to the Au Sable Point Lighthouse for us."

"Have a good day," the ranger added, as they all headed out to the car.

"No more drama or we're heading home," Mom warned.

Ben, Bekka and Eli could only look at each other. They had a feeling the drama was only beginning.

Chapter 18

Changing out of flip-flops into tennis shoes, Bekka asked her mother if she and the boys could start down the trail toward the lighthouse. They were anxious to get going.

"Sure, but don't forget your camera. I know you'll want pictures of Lake Superior from the top of the lighthouse. Dad and I have to check what food we need from the store." Bekka grabbed her camera from the table and headed off to tell the boys they could go now.

"Oh yes, tell the boys to stay on the path and not go down by the lake," her Mom added.

"I will." Bekka knew her mother was concerned for their safety. The boys had gone to the play area to hang out, so soon all three were headed down the dirt path to the lighthouse.

Sometimes it felt good to do things on their own without adults being with them. This was one of those times. They took the walk at their own pace. Ben and Bekka told Eli about the animal with the long tail, so all three looked through the underbrush, hoping to see another one cross their path.

"It was really cool," Ben started to explain. "I've never seen anything like it."

"Ow!" yelled Eli and Ben, almost at the same time.

Bekka was bent over to get a picture of a wildflower when she heard them yell. She turned just as they fell.

64

"What happened?" she exclaimed.

"Something tripped us," Ben answered, rubbing his bare leg. "Eli, did you see anything there?"

"No, but my leg has a red mark on it."

"Mine, too," Ben said, looking at his leg closely.

Bekka knelt down to get a look at the red streak.

"Bekka, did you see it happen?" Eli asked.

"No, I was taking a picture, but turned when you yelled, and then I saw you two fall down."

"It was like someone tripped us. Like someone set a trap across the trail," Ben said getting up. "Let's look and see what it was." All three looked among nearby trees for a clue.

It didn't take long for Eli to spot something tied around a tree on one side. He couldn't believe it.

"Look, there's fishing line tied to this tree, not too far from the ground. We must have fallen for someone's trap."

Following Eli's lead, Ben looked across the path from that point and found another tree with fishing line wrapped and tied around it.

"It looks like it was deliberately put here to trip some-one. Do you think it was meant for us? Do you suppose the man heard us talking last night about going to the lighthouse this morning?" Eli asked.

"I think they're trying to scare us out of here, so we won't see them do anything again. I'm not afraid of them. I'm staying. And if we catch the crooks too, then good!"

Chapter 19

"Yeah, that goes for me too," Eli said, walking on toward the lighthouse. "Let's not tell anyone about this. If our parents think we're in danger, they'd make us go home. We need to outsmart these guys at their own game."

Bekka looked back to see the adults walking quickly to catch up. "Here they come. Act as if nothing happened."

Seagulls floated over head, soaring in the wind. Then the three watched them dive straight down into the lake and come up with fish in their mouths. Other gulls screeched and dove, creating a loud racket. Sometimes it looked like two were going down for the same fish.

Before they knew it, they were at the lighthouse, arriving just as a tour was beginning, so joined the group. Ben looked around for the lady who used to live there, but she wasn't there. The tour guide told plenty of stories about the lighthouse and those who were the lightkeepers. She encouraged everyone to go upstairs and look around. Before he did, Ben tested the steps to make sure they were sturdy enough to hold him. He didn't trust anything that was one hundred thirty-five years old. The guide assured him that many men much heavier than him climbed them each year, and no one had fallen through yet. Bekka got plenty of pictures, then wandered around the lightkeeper's house imagining herself living there in the olden days before there were electric lights or a road to get into town. She would have missed having her friends live down the street.

No wonder that lady wanted friends to stay over-night, Bekka thought. *I'd be lonely too.*

Ben and Eli stood at the windows looking out over Lake Superior. The guide told stories of shipwrecks down below the cliff on which the lighthouse stood.

"The Sitka and Gale Staples both sank out here on the reef; the Sitka went down in 1904 and the Gale Staples in 1910. Wreckage can still be seen right out there in the shallow water one hundred years later."

"Let's go outside and get a better look," Eli suggested to Ben and Bekka. He had seen enough.

Turning to his father, he asked if they could go out while the adults looked at the old pictures on the walls. After getting permission, the three kids headed out with a stiff warning to be careful. The ground was uneven with prickly grass growing in the sandy soil. Even though they had been warned to stay a safe distance back, the boys got dangerously close to the edge to see what was below them. Bekka stayed a safer distance away. Crawling on their knees and looking over the edge, the boys could see the outline of ships under the water. Following along the cliff which turned to the right, the boys looked down over the edge. Ben jumped back in amazement and crouched down farther. He touched Eli's arm and put his finger to his lips, pulling Eli down too. He signaled Bekka to get down, but to hurry over with her camera. He kept his finger to his lips. He told them to slowly look over the edge.

Chapter 20

"It's a camouflage canoe," Bekka blurted out. Two men were in the canoe, paddling right below them.

"Shhh!" Ben cautioned her. "Your voice will carry and they'll know we are on to them."

"Do you think it's the guys who were in the canoe last night? I bet they think no one can see them and they're stealing stuff out of the water right under the lighthouse keeper's nose." Bekka could hardly keep from getting hysterical.

"Do you think they're the ones who put the fishing line across the path to trip us?" asked Eli.

"I'll bet they did," concluded Ben.

A brilliant idea hit Bekka. "They know what we look like, but we don't know what they look like. How about if we take their picture from up here?"

"Give me your camera, and I'll crawl to the edge over there and get it when they round the bend," her brother offered.

Thinking it a good idea, Bekka took the strap from around her neck. "Just don't drop it over the edge."

"Trust me," he said with a half-smile on his face, as he crawled away, scratching his legs on the rough grass.

"Make sure you get their faces," Eli half-whispered, crawling over by Ben. "We might need to identify them. Ow, this grass pricks my leg." Rubbing his leg where the fishing line had left a red mark made it feel even worse.

Trying to time it just right so he'd get their faces, Ben reached his hand over the edge and took a couple pictures. He couldn't be sure what he got in each one, but it was worth a try.

Just as he pulled the camera back, he heard his mother's voice call from the lighthouse steps, "Ben, get up off the ground and get back from that edge! Eli, I imagine your father wants you to come back alive too." Both boys scrambled to their feet, far enough from the edge so they couldn't be seen from the canoe on the water.

"Wow, that was close," Bekka said, running over to Ben. "If Mom had come out a minute earlier, you wouldn't have gotten a picture. How did they turn out?" She took her camera and looked into the review box. In the bright sunlight, she couldn't be sure if Ben got their faces or not. They would have to be printed out to be sure.

As Mom got closer, she looked at the boys' legs. "That grass must really be rough. Look at your legs. You've got quite the scratches on your shins. I'm surprised you aren't howling yet, Ben."

Not letting on how they really got those scratches, the boys acted tough, much to Mom's surprise. Ben was known to be rather dramatic when he got even a little scratch.

"Oh, I'll survive," he replied. His legs did hurt, but he wasn't saying a word in case Mom should head for the first-aid kit. He hated antiseptic sprays - they stung!

The men stood talking to the tour guide at the base of the lighthouse discussing the changes that had been made since the light station had opened. Mom had no idea why Ben, Eli, and Bekka smiled mischievously at each other.

Keeping his promise, on the way back to the campsite, Mr. Hartley brought up the idea of teaching Ben and Bekka how to kayak. He talked about water safety, the rule of sitting still, not tipping the kayak side to side, and more. They only half-listened as they kept looking for the camouflage canoe in the breaks between the bushes along the lake. They didn't want to appear too obvious they were looking for something, but the kids hoped they could catch up to it and get a good look at the men's faces. Realizing the canoe was too far ahead of them, they turned their attention to what Mr. Hartley was saying.

"The most important thing to remember is to remain calm, no matter what happens. Don't freak out if the kayak teeters back and forth. We have a friend named Kyla, who went out with her mother on a river near here. As they were paddling, Kyla looked down, saw a spider crawling around her seat and began to freak out, screaming like a little girl. She flipped the kayak upside-down, and they both fell out into the river."

With a wink in his eye, he said to Bekka, "You wouldn't do that, would you? I really don't want to go swimming in that cold lake." The boys started howling, picturing in their minds a dad and sister soaking wet.

Chapter 21

Kayaking proved to be easy and fun. As Ben and Bekka took their turns, Mr. Hartley explained how to keep their balance while getting in, and how to paddle.

"This is different than canoeing because you use both ends of the paddle. Hold the paddle in the middle with both hands," he said demonstrating. "Put the left end down in the water on the left side of the kayak, and then put the right end down as you paddle on the right side. You'll catch on quickly, I'm sure."

Both were scared of flipping over within the first two minutes, but soon they were moving around the shallow water like professionals. Mr. Hartley took each of them farther out into Lake Superior with its strong wind and swift current. It was hard on their arm muscles, but they agreed their family should rent two kayaks, so they all could try it.

Eli wanted to kayak with Ben, but Mr. Hartley knew it wasn't safe for them to be alone on Lake Superior. He did agree to let them try it in the Hurricane River, which is very shallow. They had so much fun, they didn't want to quit.

"I'll watch you for a few minutes to make sure you're okay, and then I'll go check my supplies for the hobo dinners. Bekka, why don't you act as the official photographer and get their picture in the kayak?"

"Okay," she said.

"Boys, make sure Bekka gets a turn, too."

"Okay," both said at the same time.

The more Mr. Hartley watched them, the more he felt they could be trusted to paddle around and stay in the river. "Just stay in the river and bring the kayak back with you when you're done."

"We will," Eli promised.

"This is fun," Ben said, grinning from ear to ear.

Bekka took pictures of them and then turned her attention to a mushroom shelf growing on the side of a tree. She walked along the edge of the river as the guys paddled alongside. The water was so clear, she could see a school of tiny little fish swimming around the canoe.

Fascinated by the fish, Ben quit paddling and leaned overboard. "Hey, there's a big ring of some kind down there. See it?"

Eli saw it too. "Hey, I think it's part of a shipwreck. I could almost reach over and get it, but I won't. I don't want to get in trouble with the ranger. Your mother would really freak out then. Let's keep on paddling."

Bekka got a picture since it looked like it was a treasure from a ship. She wanted a turn to kayak too, so the boys said they'd pull over to the side in a couple minutes and switch out. She walked along the edge as they paddled farther up the river. She didn't see a mucky hole ahead and stepped into it, losing her tennis shoe.

"Guys, slow down, I lost my shoe." Just then, she lost her balance and her foot landed right in the mud.

"Oh yuck, my sock is all mud too," she moaned.

Looking for a tree to lean against as she put her tennis shoe back on, her eyes focused on an unbelievable sight ahead of her. Not fifteen feet away, turned upside down, in a dense area of trees and bushes, was a camouflage canoe!

"Ben, Eli! There's a camouflage canoe under those bushes!"

"What?" Ben called back to her.

Realizing the owners might be close by, she didn't yell again, but put on her shoe and ran to where Ben and Eli had stopped to wait for her.

I found a camouflage canoe, and it's tipped upside-down," she all but whispered, looking back over her shoulder.

"Where?" Eli asked.

"Right over there under those bushes. I bet this is a hiding place. No one can see it from the campsites and those guys can come back and get it at night. We have to get out of here before they see us."

"Wait a minute," Ben said. "Before we go back, take a picture of the canoe so we can prove it was here. We might need it to show the ranger, so he'll know we are telling the truth."

Bekka ran back, her muddy sock making her foot slosh around in her shoe. She took several pictures, up close and then standing back by the river. Then she ran down the path next to the river while the boys paddled the kayak back to where they had put it into the river.

She arrived at the campsite wide-eyed and breath-less. Opening the door to the camper she called, "Mom, Dad, where are you? I have something amazing to tell you."

Neither parent was there. Looking around, she spotted her mother coming out of the bathhouse with a towel wrapped around her hair.

"Bekka, what is it?"

Not wanting anyone to hear, she ran across to her mother and breathlessly told her the whole story ending, "And we found a canoe, a camouflage canoe, hidden under some bushes back from the river. I'm sure it's the crooks', I just know it has to be!"

"It sounds suspicious, doesn't it?"

"I took lots of pictures in case we need to prove it was there. Where's Dad?"

"He and Mr. Hartley went to buy bait for fishing."

"Aw, we wanted them to go back and see the canoe with us."

Just then the boys came running over to them.

"Where's Dad?" Ben asked, totally out of breath from running and dragging the kayak.

"Out buying bait with Eli's dad. They thought you might like to go fishing tonight."

"Did Bekka tell you about the canoe? We wanted Dad and Mr. Hartley to go look at it with us. When will they be back?"

"I'm not sure. I need to get aluminum foil for tonight's dinner. How about if we go to a store in Grand Marais for foil and print out some of Bekka's pictures? Eli, your dad wants some to show your uncle. We won't be gone long. Give me a minute to comb my hair and we'll head out."

Mom put her hair in a ponytail and pulled on a hat. Grabbing her purse, she unlocked the car for the kids.

The trip to Grand Marais took them on back roads through a wildlife preserve, providing them with lots of entertainment. A family of ducks crossed the road in front of their car; a raccoon waddled halfway across and then turned around; and a flock of geese flew overhead in a V-formation, honking as they went.

"In one of my brochures," Mom began, "I saw a picture of something most unusual that I thought you might like to stand next to for a picture before we print them out." She couldn't help smiling as she parked in the space in front of it.

The Pickle Barrel

"What is that?" Ben asked, before laughing at it.

"It's a pickle-barrel house," Mom replied. "A man really built it for his wife. Let's go read the information signs."

"This is awesome," Bekka said, looking at the huge round house shaped just like a brown pickle barrel.

After a few good laughs about sourpusses living in a pickle barrel, Mom decided it was time to go.

"Pick a spot to stand by and I'll take your picture. Just say fuzzy pickle." Distorting their voices and their faces, they all said "fuzzy pickle" as she snapped the picture. "Great, now we can go print these out at the drugstore and pick up foil at the same time."

Hurrying down the street, they entered the store and headed for the photo department.

Looking up at the aisle markers, Mom said, "Boys, please go to aisle five and find a roll of aluminum foil for me. Bekka and I will choose which pictures we want."

"Can we each get a bag of M&Ms?" Ben asked.

"Sure. Get six bags so we can all have some," Mom said, as she took the memory card out of the camera. There were so many pictures to choose from, she decided to print them all.

"Wow, Bekka, you sure have had fun with your camera."

"Yeah, I know," she replied, grinning. She had a few surprises too, having taken pictures of the boys fooling around when they didn't know it. Boys could be so weird!

The photo machine started spitting out pictures, and soon Mom scooped them up in a pile. The boys showed up with the foil and their candy.

"We'll look at these later when our hands are clean," Mom said. "There's nothing like a picture with someone's chocolatey fingerprint in the middle of it. All right, back to the car and beyond," she said, putting her wallet back into her bag after paying for their items.

The trip back into Pictured Rocks National Park was a quiet one, as three kids popped candy into their mouths. Mom enjoyed the peace and quiet, while the unopened packet of pictures filled Bekka's mind with questions. *Did they get a good picture of the men's faces? Would a canoe hiding under bushes prove anything? Would they be heroes for stopping the theft of maritime artifacts?*

Chapter 22

Ben and Eli's plan to go back to the canoe was put on hold when they saw their dads working on the campfire.

"Hi guys, it's almost time to make the hobo dinners," Mr. Hartley called to them, as they got out of the car.

Looking around, Eli spoke softly, "But, Dad, we have something really important to show you."

"Can it wait?" his dad asked. "These have to get cooking, and then we'll have plenty of daylight left to do whatever it is you want."

"I guess," he said.

Seeing the ingredients for the dinners on the table made Eli forget about a canoe under a bush. Ben and Bekka were going to be amazed at what they were about to eat.

Looking at their hands, Mom cut in, "Nobody handles any food until those hands are good and clean. I think I see river algae on them." Flipping their hands over to see if they had turned green, the three of them headed for the bathhouse.

"Race ya," Ben said, and took off.

Racing into the bathhouse, he almost ran down a man coming out. Embarrassed, he kept his head down and said a quick, "Sorry". Bekka watched it happen and giggled as she went into the women's restroom.

Five minutes later, the process of making dinner was about to begin. Piles of food were on the table.

"Eli, would you like the honor of explaining how to assemble a hobo dinner?" his dad asked when everyone was back at their picnic table.

"Yeah," he said, grinning from ear to ear. "First you take a hunk of ground meat and flatten it into a hamburger. Then you lay it in the middle of a piece of foil. Next you layer on some onions, sliced potatoes, and some of these baby carrots. Some people like to put salt and pepper on theirs. I don't, I put on lots of ketchup when it is done cooking."

"Sweet," Bekka said, neatly laying her burger on the foil. "Do we have to eat onions?" Bekka wrinkled her nose.

"No," said her mother, "but you do have to have carrots and potatoes. Have you had your five fruits and vegetables today?" She laughed at her own question.

Eli continued his explanation. "Now, after your food is stacked on top of each other, bring the edges of the foil together, roll it down and fold over the ends like this."

Walking over to the campfire with his foil packet, Mr. Hartley said, "To cook them, we'll lay them in the coals near the edges so they cook slowly. They need heat under and around them, but you don't want to put them into a blazing hot fire." He used a pancake turner to position his just right.

"They'll take a little while to cook, so let's get out our fishing poles and check our lines and lures while they cook." He stood up and reached for his favorite rod.

"Most likely, they will be done when we are through putting on the hooks. The lake is good for fishing in the evening when the water is calmer. As a surprise, we rented two boats for tonight."

"Wow, Dad! That's cool," Eli said, excited about what their dads did to surprise them.

"I'm not putting worms on my hook," Bekka declared. "Feeling them crawl on my fingers gives me the creeps. E-w-w!" At that, her whole body shuddered.

"I don't blame you," Mom chimed in, "I don't like that squishy feeling either."

"Girls," Ben said with disgust. "It's a good thing you don't have to catch our supper."

Wrapping a worm around a hook didn't bother him a bit. He hadn't been fishing for a long time. This was going to be fun. Vacations were the best.

Dad and Mr. Hartley got out the poles, pulled on the fishing line, and checked the tackle boxes to be sure there were enough bobbers, lures, and bait.

Dad stood four poles up next to the camper. "This looks very promising, I can almost smell the fish frying in our pan already. How about a fish-fry tomorrow night? Whoever catches the most fish doesn't have to clean any!" He called out the challenge to everyone.

"D-a-a-d," Bekka said, turning toward her father. Everyone turned to see what made her squeal now.

"I'm not cleaning any old fish that flips and flops."
Just the thought of it sent another shudder down her spine.

"Well, we'll make an exception to that rule," he said.
He couldn't help but wink at his daughter.

"Make that two exceptions to the rule," Mom said,
stepping over to put an arm around her daughter. "We
girls have to stick together. I tried filleting fish once, and
it freaked me out. I cut off the head and the tail flipped
up. The next fish, I cut off the tail and the head flipped up.
I screamed and quit right then and there. I like to buy my
fish ready-to-eat." The boys were laughing their heads off
imagining Mom screaming at a little fish.

"Hey," exclaimed Mr. Hartley, dashing over to the
fire as steam rose from the foil packet dinners. "I think our
dinners are done."

With the flipper, he carefully lifted the packets off the
coals, making sure he didn't rip them open. Ben ran into
the camper for the bottle of ketchup and then settled into
his seat on the bench for a delightful meal.

"What's really neat about these meals is that you eat
them right in the foil, so there's no cleanup needed," Mr.
Hartley said, as he unrolled his foil.

"I like this idea," Mom said, relieved there wouldn't be
a stack of dishes or pots and pans to wash.

Anxious to begin eating his, Ben reached for his.

"Hot!" he exclaimed, using his fingertips to open it.
Despite slightly burned fingers, the smell made him melt.

"Sorry. I forgot to warn you to be careful. The foil holds the heat and will be hot," apologized Mr. Hartley.

The rest of the meal was spent almost in silence as everyone enjoyed their food.

"Dad, can we do these at home in our grill?" asked Ben. "These are so good."

"I think we can. We'll try it next weekend. Now, what was it you wanted to talk to us about when you got back from town? Or have you forgotten what it was?"

Chapter 23

Eli started the story. Bekka looked down at her sock.

"Dad, remember how you told us to stay in the river with the kayak and not go into the lake? Well, we decided to paddle farther up the river, away from Lake Superior. It's really shallow, only a kayak could go up it. Bekka was running along the bank taking pictures of us and other stuff, and all of a sudden she stepped in some thick mud, and her shoe came off. She lost her balance and put her foot right into more mud."

All eyes turned to Bekka as they listened to Eli talk. Ben took up the story at that point. "She told us to stop, so we did, and she reached down to get her shoe and put it on, and then she looked over and saw-" Softening his voice, he leaned toward their parents so no one beyond their campsite could hear, "she saw a camouflage canoe."

"Yeah, it was upside-down under some bushes," Bekka added.

"That's curious," Dad said, looking out toward the woods. "Why would anyone hide a canoe in those woods?"

"I got a picture of it," Bekka said proudly, "and Mom had them printed out when we went to buy the foil."

"That's right," exclaimed Mom standing up. "I'll get those pictures so we can look at them. We didn't look at them in the car because we were eating M&Ms." Off she went to the camper to get them.

There were about fifty pictures in the packet and everyone teased Bekka for being such a shutterbug.

"Hey, I like to take pictures. It's fun," she said good-naturedly, as she blushed.

The boys laughed when they saw the ones she took of them fooling around on the monkey bars and paddling the kayak. And they mocked the one of her mushroom shelf on the pine tree. Soon the kidding turned serious as they saw the pictures of the men in the canoe and those of the canoe under the bushes.

Picking up the one with the men's faces, Bekka exclaimed, "Hey, that's the man you bumped into tonight at the bathhouse, Ben."

"Let me see," Ben said, grabbing for the picture. He couldn't believe he had been that close to one of the bad guys.

"If these men are doing something illegal, you have proof of what they and their canoe look like," Dad said. "How about showing us where you found the canoe?"

"We know right where it is," Eli said, jumping up from the table.

"I'll clear up dinner while you detectives go find that canoe," Mom said.

No one refused that offer and were off to discover a hidden canoe. Retracing her steps, Bekka walked close to the water looking for the spot where her shoe made an indentation in the mud.

She found the location and then looked for the tree she was leaning against when she saw the canoe. Positioning herself as she was before, she looked in the direction of the canoe. She was sure she was aimed in the right direction, but when they walked over to the bushes, the canoe was gone!

Chapter 24

"It's gone, Dad!" Ben couldn't believe his eyes. "It was right here. You saw the pictures."

"Yes, we did."

"Do you think someone was watching us and moved it before we came back?" Eli asked.

Ben had another idea.

"Do you think they plan to strike again tonight?"

"They just might," Dad said in a tone that reassured the kids he believed their story. "We'll have to keep an eye out for them tonight while we are out fishing. They have to return sometime."

Bekka beamed when she heard her father say, "Your camera sure came in handy today. The pictures may help identify the canoe, should we need to."

Noticing the sun was getting closer to the horizon, Mr. Hartley said, "Since we can't do anything more here, let's go fishing and catch some of that trout Lake Superior is famous for."

"Yeah!" sounded three excited voices.

Steering clear of muddy spots, Bekka led the way back to the campsite. She went straight for her camera, strapped it around her neck and went to get her fishing pole. She liked to fish- she just didn't want to touch a creepy crawly worm.

"Bekka is a sissy," taunted Ben, as he and Eli passed her on the trail to the lake.

"I am not! I just don't like worms. I bet I can catch more fish than you can," she challenged, as she ran past the boys.

"Oh yeah? How much you wanna bet?" Ben challenged her back.

"One week's allowance," she said, walking backwards, putting her chin in the air.

"You're on!"

After bringing down the boats, Dad said, "Ben, you're in the boat with Eli and his dad. Bekka, you're here with us." Mom handed out life jackets. They divided the worms and soon were rowing out into the lake.

"This is a perfect night for fishing. The lake is calm and the sun still has a couple hours before setting," said Mr. Hartley, looking west across Lake Superior.

Without teasing her, Dad put Bekka's worm on her hook, and she cast the line into the water. Ben and Eli dug right into their worm container, looking for nice fat ones. They pushed them on the hooks like they were old pros and cast their lines way out into the lake. Then they waited for a fish to take their bait. A family of ducks swam by and then a family of loons. Every once in awhile, a loon dove into the water and came up with a fish.

"I think we'll row over there since they seem to be getting fish," Mr. Hartley said, putting his oars into the water. Dad did the same and much to their amazement, soon fish were filling their buckets.

Wanting to win this bet, Bekka kept quiet about how many fish she caught, even though Ben called out each and every time he dropped one into the bucket. She tried to stay one fish ahead of him. Counting the number of fish in their bucket, Dad realized they had caught their legal limit and declared they were done for the day.

"I won! I won!" Bekka all but shouted. "I got five and you got four, Ben."

"Did she really get five?" he asked, not wanting to believe he had lost to his sister.

"I'm afraid so," replied their mother.

"I won fair and square," taunted Bekka. "You can give me your five dollars at any time."

"Did she cheat?"

"No, she won fair and square. And now, we get to clean these beauties," Dad said, holding up a string of lake trout. "Eli, you ever clean a fish?"

"No,"

"Well, you're about to learn. We'll come back for the boats when we are done cleaning the trout."

They rowed back to the beach and pulled the boats up onto the shore. The three young fishermen posed for a picture with their strings of fish. It was a proud day for Bekka.

The sun was setting as they finished cleaning the last fish at the Hartley's picnic table. Ben and Eli tried their hand at cutting off the heads and tails, and let their dads slice them into thin fillets.

Not wanting to appear to be a sissy, Bekka offered to wrap the fish in foil when they were done. The roll of foil was still on their picnic table from dinner, so she ran over to get it. As she picked up the box, a piece of paper fell on the ground. Bending over to pick it up, she knew it said something, but in the dim light, she couldn't read it. Who would have left them a note? Getting a flashlight, she looked at it and froze. Another warning:

"We know who you are.
Mind your own business or else!"

She screamed her famous scream. It broke the quietness of the campground. Forgetting about the foil, she ran over to the Hartley's campsite with the note.

"What happened?" asked Mom, looking back at their camper to see what had frightened her daughter.

She showed her mother the note, who read it out loud. Ben, Bekka, and Eli looked at each other. The men must know they had found the canoe. A creepy, scary feeling went down their spines. They were dealing with serious adults capable of doing serious harm.

"Now what?" Mom asked, upset because they were being watched by criminals.

"I'm not sure," Dad replied, "but this means another trip to the ranger's station tomorrow. He wanted us to let him know if something else happened."

Chapter 25

In all their excitement, everyone forgot the rowboats until after dark. Ben, Bekka, and Eli trudged to the beach with their fathers to load them into Mr. Hartley's truck. The men carried the boats while the boys followed with the oars. Bekka guided them with a flashlight. Just for fun, Ben and Eli tried lifting one end of a boat. They couldn't budge it.

"This is heavier than it looks," Eli said. They were amazed at their fathers' strength. Bending down, they picked up the wet and sandy oars and loaded them in the truckbed.

"My hands are all gritty from the sand," Eli said. "Can we go wash them in the lake while you tie down the boats?"

"Sure," Mr. Hartley said, tightening a knot.

Offering to lead with her flashlight, Bekka and the boys dashed to rinse their hands in the water. The moon cast a bright white beam across Lake Superior. It was something none of the kids had ever seen before. Bekka shut off her light and they stood there for a few minutes in the dark. Wiping wet hands on their pants, the threesome turned to go back up the trail, but froze in their tracks. A canoe came out of nowhere, gliding silently across the lake. With just the moonlight guiding their way, the canoe passed where the kids stood. Bekka touched her brother's arm and immediately he put his hand over her mouth.

"Shhh!" Ben whispered. "They don't know we're here. Let's see what they do." Crouching down on their heels, the three would have looked like big boulders, had someone been able to see them.

Canoe paddles silently moved in and out of the water and stopped a short distance from them. Eli touched Ben's arm and pointed up the shoreline. Someone farther up the beach was flashing a light toward the canoe. Then came a splash as someone dove into the water. Bekka had an overwhelming desire to scream, so she put her own hand over her mouth.

Within a minute, they heard something that sounded like metal hitting the bottom of the canoe, and then they heard another splash. In almost no time, they heard the sound of more metal being put into the canoe. Not knowing they were being watched, the men talked about the objects they were hauling out of the water.

"They're stealing parts of the shipwrecks," Eli said.

"What should we do?" asked Ben.

"What can we do?" asked his friend back.

"If we yell at them, they'll know we're here and they might do something to us while we're sleeping," added Bekka. "Remember the note? They know who we are." Now she was really scared.

"Somehow we have to set a trap to catch them with the stolen stuff. Besides, Mom will insist we go home if she thinks they will do something to us," Ben said. His mind swirled with many thoughts. They had to think fast.

"What kind of a trap could we set?" asked Eli.

"Give me a minute to think. What do we have that we could use on them?" Ben answered back.

"I have an idea," Bekka said. "But we have to sneak back up the beach and set the trap." She quietly explained her idea, and together they worked out the plan.

"We're going to have to stay in the shadows. Don't make a sound or that guy on the beach will know it is us," Ben warned.

Slowly, very slowly they made their way over rocks and sandy areas until they reached the path to the campsite. They knew if they told their parents what was happening, they wouldn't be able to leave the campsite to set the trap, so they would have to act like nothing happened.

Chapter 26

Mr. and Mrs. Cooper were enjoying the campfire when the three walked up to the campsite. Mr. Hartley was reading a book in his tent.

"Hi, there, want to make a s'more?" asked Mom.

"Ah, no thanks, not right now," Ben said. "We want to take a little walk. It's fun walking in the moonlight, but we'll take a flashlight with us." He went into the camper and got one as well as a knife.

"Don't go too far," Dad said. "It's getting a little late."

"We'll be careful," Bekka said, grabbing her secret weapon, which neither parent noticed. They walked in the opposite direction of the lake and disappeared from sight.

They knew where they had to go, and they only had a short time to work their plan. The moonlight replaced the flashlight. If someone heard a noise, they might think it was just a raccoon or deer. But if they saw a flashlight, they might come to investigate.

"Do you really think this will work?" Eli asked a few minutes later, tying a knot as tightly as he could. His heart beat wildly. This was the most dangerous thing he had ever done.

"It worked once, and it should this time, too," Bekka said with confidence. She bent down to check that the knot was tight enough. She helped Eli get everything in the right position and then walked over by her brother. "Let's get out of here."

96

As they arrived at their campsite, Dad was putting another log on the fire. Mr. Hartley had joined them for a late-night snack.

"Hi, there. We were beginning to wonder if we should send out a search party," Mom said.

The three of them looked at each other, smiling in the dark. Had it been daytime, Mom would have seen guilty looks on their faces and asked a zillion questions.

"Want a s'more?" Dad asked. "If so, you'd better hurry, the marshmallows are going fast."

"Please say no," Eli's dad said, teasing them. He pulled two golden marshmallows off his skewer.

"No way," Eli said, "back away from the marshmallows and no one will get hurt."

All three kids took skewers and slid marshmallows onto them. They were bursting inside wanting to tell what they had just done, but they didn't. Soon the crooks would be walking right into their trap.

All three had a hard time going to sleep. Their minds kept imagining what might be happening outside. Would the crooks come looking for them, or would they leave in the night? First thing in the morning, they would check their trap.

Chapter 27

Eli was the first to wake the next morning. Crawling into his jeans, he asked himself many questions. *What if the crooks didn't set off the trap? If the canoe wasn't theirs, whose was it? Why would they steal so many things from the shipwrecks? Were they dangerous people?*

He finished dressing. Butterflies filled his stomach. He would go over and see if Ben and Bekka were awake. How could they sleep at a time like this?

"Eli, what are you doing?" his father asked, rousing from his sleep and looking at his watch. "It's only 7:30. Nobody's awake. Do you hear anyone outside anywhere?"

"I just can't sleep. I thought I would go see if Ben and Bekka are awake. Maybe we can take a walk or play on the monkey bars," he reasoned with his father.

"How about reading a book?"

"Dad, it's summer vacation."

"Oh, yeah, I forgot," Dad said with a half-grin. "If you go over to their camper, listen first. If you don't hear voices, come back."

"Okay," he said, unzipping the flap of their tent and looking around. "You know, Dad, tents aren't really safe, are they? I think we should get a camper."

"Our tent is just fine. If we don't bother anyone, they won't bother us."

"Good," Eli said, as he stepped outside. It was a little chilly, so he was glad he chose his jeans and a sweatshirt.

Over in the camper, Ben was also awake. His mind raced with thoughts of what had happened since they left Lansing. Meeting Eli and his father was fun. It gave them someone new to do things with, and who knew, maybe they could see Eli when they returned home. Rolling over in his sleeping bag, he thought he heard a ping. Then he heard it again. Was it chipmunks dropping acorns on their camper? No, the sound wasn't coming from the roof, something was hitting his end of the camper. He moved the curtain aside to see what animal was out there and saw Eli. He couldn't believe he was already dressed.

What is he doing out there so early? Is he as excited as I am?

Ben got really close to the window and mouthed something Eli couldn't understand, but at least Eli knew he was awake. Eli motioned for Ben to come outside.

Ben grabbed for his jeans and a jacket, quietly unlocked the door, and stepped outside.

"Why are you up so early?" Ben asked, rubbing his eyes in the early morning sunlight.

"I'm so excited, I just can't sleep. I want to go look at our trap right now."

"We can't go without Bekka. She'd be mad at us."

"Yeah, I know. Do you think you could go in and make some noise to wake her up?"

"No, but we could throw some of these little pine cones at her window and see if she wakes up. Besides, I'm hungry."

"Me, too," said Eli, rubbing his stomach. They were too excited last night to eat more than one s'more, and now their stomachs were empty.

"Ben, what are you and Eli doing out there?" Dad whispered from the doorway.

"Oh, we're just talking. We're hungry. What's good for breakfast?"

"Cereal. We want to go to the Log Slide and do another nature hike for your Junior Ranger books, so we'll do an easy breakfast."

"Can we get our own food if we're quiet?" Ben asked. His father's voice woke up Bekka. She came and stood beside her dad, wondering who he was talking to. She hadn't heard Ben get up.

"Hey, what are you guys doing?" she asked.

"Nothing, just talking," her brother answered back.

"I'm coming out too," she said, hustling to get on her clothes. She didn't want them sneaking off without her.

"Well, if everyone is awake, we might as well get an early start to our day," Dad declared. "I'll hand you out the cereal and milk and you guys can eat."

"I'll go get my cereal," Eli said. "We have granola."

"That sounds good. Can I have some too?"

"Sure."

The boys each devoured a heaping bowlful of cereal by the time Bekka appeared, and were about to fill their bowls again.

"Hey, save me some," she begged.

"Sorry, too late," Ben teased. He made it look like the box was empty.

"Not fair," she whined.

"Just kidding," her brother said, handing her the box.

"When do you think we should go to you-know-where?" Eli asked, lowering his voice, leaning toward Ben.

"After we finish eating. Our parents haven't eaten, so maybe we have time before we leave," Bekka replied.

They couldn't act too suspicious, but they needed time to check the trap. All three finished eating and cleared the table. They didn't want their parents calling them back.

"Can we take a walk while you guys eat?" Ben asked his parents, opening the camper door.

"Are you done already?" Mom asked. She looked at the clock and said, "Okay, you can go, but we're going to the Log Slide shortly, so don't be gone too long."

"We won't," Bekka said. She and Ben took off for the Hartley's tent to see if Eli could go too.

He was rolling up his sleeping bag when they arrived. He flopped over the top of the roll, trying to grab the strings. He wished he had octopus arms sometimes.

"Can you go?" Ben called to Eli through the tent opening.

"Yeah, when I get my sleeping bag rolled up."

"Can we help?" asked Bekka. She was anxious to get going.

"I'm almost done. Trying to tie these strings," Eli replied, yanking on a short string to make it longer. After another try at it, he got it tied together and rolled it into a corner out of the way. Tents never had enough room for people to walk in.

Stepping outside, the three looked around for any strangers. Not seeing anyone, they took off for Hurricane River, wondering if the canoe would be back under the bushes and if treasures might be hidden under it.

"What'll we do if the men see us snooping around?" Eli asked.

"We'll just say we are looking for a good place to kayak and keep walking by the river. If they chase us, just run back toward the campground. Don't admit you know anything," Ben said, sounding brave.

They followed the path they had covered the last couple days, this time watching for a camouflage canoe lying anywhere. They also looked for the metal ring they'd seen yesterday on the riverbed, but it was gone.

"I bet they came back and got it," Bekka said.

"Wow," Eli said. "If they get caught, they're going to be in so much trouble."

As they got closer to the trap, they walked faster. Their curiosity was getting the best of them.

"It worked!" Bekka exclaimed, when they reached where they had set their trap. "It worked. They fell for our trap." She jumped up and down and talked so loudly, Ben thought she could be heard a mile away.

"Shhh! Someone will hear you and come over to see what's going on," her brother scolded.

"But they fell for it, they fell for it!" she said over and over.

"Now what?" asked Eli.

"I'm not sure, but they are the guilty ones," Ben declared. "Let's go back and tell our parents we need to see the ranger before more treasure is stolen or the bad guys get away."

Chapter 28

"What's wrong with you two?" Dad asked Ben and Bekka when they reached the campsite. "You're acting like you have ants in your pants." They just couldn't hold in their secret much longer. They had so much to tell a ranger.

All six of them piled into the Coopers' car after making bologna and cheese sandwiches for a picnic lunch. The plan was to go to the Ranger's Station to show them the latest note and then go to the Log Slide. As they drove, Mom told again how loggers used sand dunes to slide giant pine trees down the log slide to the lake below. She wanted the kids to know what they would see and also remind them of the danger in leaning too far over the three-hundred-foot dune. Bekka brought along the prints of her pictures to look at and then decide which ones to give Eli to keep.

Ten minutes later, they turned into the parking lot. They hoped Ranger Greg would be there. Dad had the note the crooks left under the roll of foil. He wanted to prove something bad was going on and that possibly they were in danger.

Getting back out of the car, Ben lost his balance and almost stumbled headlong onto the pavement. Mom let out a little scream, making Ben roll his eyes. He didn't like attention like that. Plus his nose hurt from the last fall.

Ranger Greg was outside giving directions to new

campers, so they waited for him to finish talking. He waved as the campers drove away and smiled as everyone walked up to him.

"Ranger Greg," Dad began, "we had another incident last night. Apparently something criminal is still going on and we are in the middle of it. While we were out fishing, this note was left at our campsite. We don't know what caused it, but this one is a warning."

Ben, Bekka, and Eli looked at each other. They knew why the thieves threatened them. The ranger took the note and read it, puzzled.

"It's funny, but no one else has reported anything going on. It's odd only you are getting these notes."

Bekka got the feeling he didn't believe them. Looking across the parking lot, she began to yell.

"There they are! There they are!" Her scream pierced everyone's eardrums. She pointed to a pick-up truck with a camouflage canoe in the back end.

"That's them," Ben and Eli said together.

"Who? Where? How do you know?" Ranger Greg asked anxiously.

Bekka was practically jumping up and down, pointing down the road.

"It's the camouflage canoe. You have to stop them! We have proof. Stop them!"

The ranger looked down the road and back at the Coopers and Hartleys, trying to decide what to do.

The truck was heading toward the park's exit.

"Please, please stop them," Bekka begged. "They're the bad guys."

"Are you sure?" asked Ranger Greg, looking them straight in the eyes.

"Yes!" the three said together. "We have pictures."

"Let me see," he demanded, reaching for them. Looking through the pictures quickly, he realized they were telling the truth.

By then, the truck was getting away. Ranger Greg took out his cell phone and called the ranger at the exit gate.

"Apprehend and detain a pickup with a camouflage canoe in it. Do not allow them to leave. They may have stolen artifacts. I have a carload of people who say they have proof."

"Proof?" Mr. Hartley turned and asked the kids. "What proof do we have that they are the ones we saw in the dark?"

"Trust us, Dad," Eli said. "Let's go and catch them before they get away."

"You follow me," Ranger Greg instructed, running toward his official truck. "When we get there, don't say a word. Let *me* ask the questions."

They followed closely behind the ranger's vehicle. In the Coopers' car, the parents still weren't sure what proof the kids had, but they decided to wait and see what happened. No one should get away with stealing treasures from shipwrecks.

They could tell the ranger was on his phone again. Then he hung up and sped toward the exit. Mr. Cooper drove faster, too.

"Wow! We're really speeding," Bekka said, noticing they were going faster than they ever had.

"Hang on," Dad warned. "This is as close to a police chase as we ever want to be."

Mom was about to pass out.

Chapter 29

Within minutes, they were almost to the exit of the park. The exit gate was down and a ranger stood right in front of the pickup, preventing it from leaving. Two men sat in the truck, angry looks on their faces.

Ranger Greg jumped out of his car and hurried over. The Coopers and the Hartleys kept a safe distance back in case something dangerous happened.

"Please step out of your truck," Ranger Greg said, looking sternly at the men.

"Why?" asked the driver, opening the door.

"We have a few questions to ask you."

"About what?"

Looking inside the truck, Ranger Greg told the passenger to step out of the vehicle, too. He got out and went around to the front of the truck, acting nervous. His right knee couldn't stop moving back and forth.

Looking directly at the two men, Ranger Greg said, "These people said they saw you stealing artifacts from the lake three nights ago. You also left them threatening messages several times."

"It's a lie! We did nothing like that," the driver said, getting angry. His friend fidgeted even more.

The ranger continued, "Where did you stay? Which campground? Don't lie. We have records with your license plate on it."

"Hurricane River Campground," the driver said, "but we didn't do anything wrong. We just went canoeing in the lake by the campground and up the Hurricane River."

"That's not true!" Bekka said, surprising her parents.

"How do you know that, young lady?" Ranger Greg asked, turning in her direction.

"We have pictures of them way down at the light-house. And besides, the Hurricane River is too shallow to canoe in. Only kayaks can use it."

"Well, maybe we got lost," the driver said.

"Where did you keep your canoe?"

"Right by our tent," the driver insisted.

"That's not true," Ben blurted out. "We have pictures." The men did a double take at him.

"What did you do at night?"

"Nothing; it's too dark to canoe at night," he replied.

"That's not true!" Bekka sputtered.

"Okay, that's enough," the ranger said sternly. He had to get to the bottom of these accusations. Turning to Ben, Bekka, Eli, and their parents, he said, "Start from the beginning and tell me what you saw and heard."

Dad began with the tour boat ride, seeing the men on the boat, and then recognizing them in the pictures taken at the lighthouse.

"We can't be sure who it was," he continued, "but we know someone was diving from a canoe after dark, and we surprised them on the beach."

"See, you can't prove anything," the passenger stated.

"Why did you hide your canoe?" Ranger Greg asked.

"Hide it? Why would we hide it?" the driver asked.

"You tell us," the ranger said, holding up one of Bekka's prints. "We have a picture here of your canoe hidden under bushes by the river."

"Ah, well…" he stammered, "but it doesn't prove we were stealing things out of the water!"

"We have proof," Ben stated.

"What?" the adults said together.

Much to their parents' and the ranger's shock, the kids described how they went back to the lake to wash their hands and saw the canoe come from the direction of the river. They'd heard the sounds of metal objects being put into the canoe. The more the adults heard of their adventure, the more amazed they became.

Ben bragged on his sister when he explained Bekka's plan to trap the thieves. Now their parents became alarmed at how close their children had been to danger.

Ben continued, "Bekka came up with the idea of using fishing line stretched back and forth across the river three times and tied around trees. It was dark so they couldn't see it, and low enough so it would trip them when they walked up the river to hide their canoe in the bushes."

"How did you do it without getting wet?" Mom asked.

"We rolled up our pants and walked across without getting wet. Yesterday we saw a metal ring in the water. We left it there, but it was gone this morning."

"You're just making it up. Kids aren't smart enough to do that kind of stuff!"

"Oh, yeah?" Eli fired back.

"There's proof," Bekka said again.

"What proof?" the pickup truck driver asked sarcastically.

"Roll up your pant legs. You'll prove it yourselves," Ben jumped in.

"I'm not rolling up my pants for any stinkin' kids," the passenger said. He was one stubborn dude.

Believing the kids' story, Ranger Greg demanded, "Just do it!"

Both men bent over and slowly rolled up their pant legs six inches. Much to the shock of everyone but the kids, on the legs of the two crooks were red lines – stripes going straight across. Mom put her hands to her mouth and gasped.

"They walked right into our trap," Ben gloated.

"How did you kids know how to do this?" asked the ranger.

"Well, it worked when they did it to us," Ben said, as he and Eli rolled up their jeans, displaying their red lines.

Mom let out another gasp. The two dads were ready to jump into action when they heard their kids had been victims of a trap.

"I thought you got those scratches crawling on the grass at the lighthouse," Mom said, raising an eyebrow.

"Yeah, well, you'd have made us go home, if you knew how it really happened," Bekka said, sounding guilty.

Eli's father was equally frightened for his son's safety. "Do you realize you might have been harmed if these guys caught you doing this?"

"Yeah, but we didn't want to go home early," Eli answered. "Someone had to stop them from stealing anything more from the ships."

"I think a search of this truck is in order," Ranger Greg announced. Turning to his partner, he instructed him to remove everything- and he meant everything- out of the vehicle.

"It's just our camping gear, food, and clothes," stated the driver. "Look all you want."

The ranger looked through the duffel bags and cooler; even unrolling the sleeping bags and tent to see if anything was hidden in them.

Coming up empty-handed, the ranger shrugged his shoulders. The kids almost panicked, thinking they might have accused the wrong people.

"Is there anything hiding under the canoe up there?" Ben asked, pointing to the front end of the canoe.

Ranger Greg climbed up on the back bumper, but couldn't see anything. Eli stared at the back of the truck, then spotted something.

"Hey, that's not where a spare tire usually goes," he said, thinking it odd a tire was loose in the back of the truck.

The ranger answered, "No, it's not." He bent down and looked under the back of the truck where a tire is usually kept. Stretching to look a little closer, he exclaimed, "Well, look what we have here. A metal box attached to the bottom of the truck. Clever, very clever. I do believe we have the evidence for a case of maritime artifact theft."

"Yes!" Ben said, pumping his fist in the air.

Just then a car came rumbling down the road toward the gate. When the driver saw the commotion at the gate, he slowed and then sped away.

"Dad," Ben exclaimed, "That's the guy I saw through my binoculars sending the semaphore signals. He's their partner Tom. He's getting away!"

Ranger Greg opened his cell phone, dialed 9-1-1, and gave a description of the car. He shut his phone.

"He won't get far. The police will pick him up. I think we have an open-and-shut case on this one. Thanks to three young Junior Rangers, we can retrieve the stolen property and bring these men to justice."

Chapter 30

Mr. and Mrs. Cooper and Mr. Hartley didn't know whether to scold or hug their children when Ranger Greg and his supervisor were done questioning them. The rangers kept Bekka's pictures as evidence against the men. When Mom calmed down, she told them she didn't want any more excitement, or they were going home early. This time, though, they knew she was only kidding. What could top this adventure?

The park rangers' supervisor walked them to their car, inviting them to a lunch on Friday. He told Ben, Bekka, and Eli to bring their Junior Ranger books if they were done with the assignments.

"Now before you go, I'd like to have your picture taken with me beside the Pictured Rocks National Shoreline sign. It's going on display for everyone to see."

For the rest of the afternoon, they trekked to and around the Log Slide seeing for themselves what amazing work was done by loggers using carts with twelve-foot-high wheels. Fortunately, nobody fell over the edge or required a helicopter rescue by the Coast Guard. Bekka smiled to herself, knowing Mom would not have handled it well. That evening, over a bowl of hot, buttery popcorn, the three kids worked on their books, filling in the answers and discovered the D word was diversity. They had indeed learned a lot about Pictured Rocks' animal habitats, birds, logging, and what it takes to preserve its special artifacts.

Much to their surprise, they were the guests of honor at the lunch on Friday. Bekka's pictures were on display and their heroic story was told. Newspaper reporters snapped their pictures making them the headline story, even in the *Lansing State Journal*.

Ranger Greg looked through their Junior Ranger books, stamped them, and awarded them a special patch. The supervisor shook their hands, thanked them for their bravery, and gave each one a Petoskey stone, cut in the shape of a mitten which, as everyone knows, looks like the lower peninsula of Michigan.

THE END

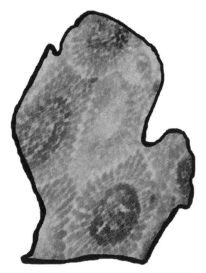

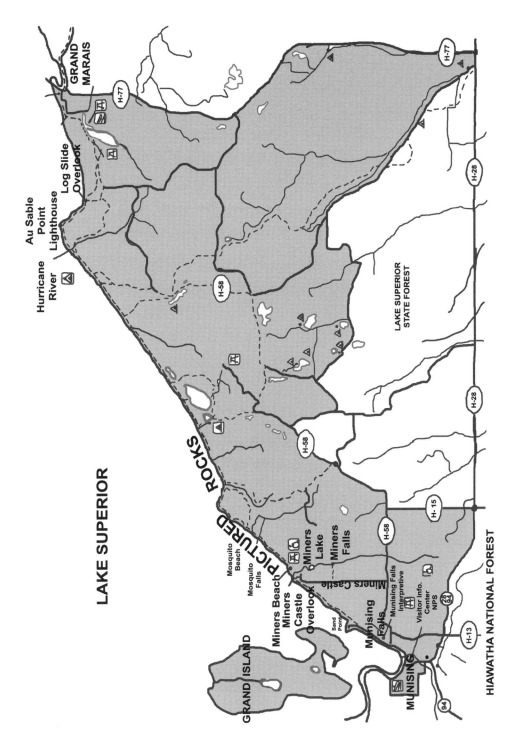

LAKE SUPERIOR

GRAND MARAIS

Au Sable Point Lighthouse

Log Slide Overlook

Hurricane River

H-77

H-77

H-28

LAKE SUPERIOR STATE FOREST

H-58

H-58

GRAND ISLAND

Miners Beach

Miners Castle Overlook

PICTURED ROCKS

Mosquito Beach

Mosquito Falls

Miners Castle

Miners Beach

Miners Lake

Miners Falls

H-58

H-15

Sand Point

Munising Falls

Munising Falls Interpretive Center

Visitor Info. Center NPS

H-58

28 94

H-13

MUNISING

94

HIAWATHA NATIONAL FOREST

Recipe for Hobo Dinners:
*serves four

With the help of an adult:
Divide one pound of ground meat into four patties
Slice up four potatoes
Peel and slice two carrots and an onion
Salt and pepper – for seasoning.

Pull off four 12 inch lengths of aluminum foil –
Layer on the meat patties and vegetables.
Salt and pepper them.
Fold up the foil and place on the coals of a campfire.
Cook 20 – 25 minutes. Flip once.

Recipe for S'mores

For each s'more you need:
1 whole graham cracker broken in half,
2 marshmallows,
and one-half of a chocolate candy bar.
Roast the marshmallows over a fire
and put them on top of a graham cracker.
Lay the chocolate candy bar on top and
cover it with the other cracker.
Enjoy!

The Song of Hiawatha

by Henry Wadsworth Longfellow

"By the shores of Gitchee Gumee,
By the shining Big-Sea-Water,
Stood the wigwam of Nokomis,
Daughter of the Moon, Nokomis.
Dark behind it rose the forest,
Rose the black and gloomy pine-trees,
Rose the firs with cones upon them;
Bright before it beat the water,
Beat the clear and sunny water,
Beat the shining Big-Sea-Water.
There the wrinkled old Nokomis,
Nursed the little Hiawatha,
Rocked him in his linden cradle,
Bedded soft in moss and rushes.
Safely bound with reindeer sinews;
Stilled his fretful wail by saying,
"Hush! The Naked Bear will hear thee!"
Lulled him into slumber,
Singing, "Ewa-yea! my little owlet!
Who is this, that lights the wigwam?
With his great eyes lights the wigwam?
Ewa-yea! my little owlet!"

LAKE SUPERIOR FACTS

Did you know:

1 - Lake Superior is the largest lake in the world. It contains as much water as all the other Great Lakes combined, plus three extra Lake Eries!

2 - The average depth is 483 feet; the deepest point is 1,333 feet.

3 - The biggest wave ever recorded was 31 feet high.

4 - There are 78 different species of fish that call the big lake home.

5 - It very rarely freezes over completely, and then usually just for a few hours. Complete freezing occurred in 1962, 1979, 2003 and 2009.

6 - In the summer, the sun sets more than 35 minutes later on the western shore of Lake Superior than at its southeastern edge.

7 - There have been about 350 shipwrecks recorded in Lake Superior.

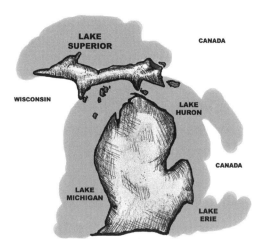

Maritime artifacts which have drifted on shore of Lake Superior.

Anchor chain on shipwreck

Boom on shipwreck

Oval ring from shipwreck

Sable Point Wreck

Staples and Sitka prior to sinking

The Semaphore Alphabet

Use the semaphore signals on the following pages to read the message from Ben and Bekka.

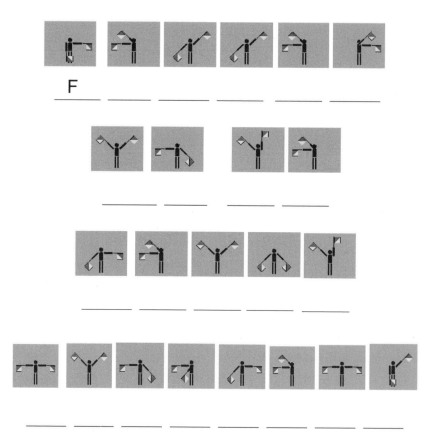

F _____ _____ _____ _____ _____

_____ _____ _____ _____

_____ _____ _____

_____ _____ _____ _____ _____

A and 1 (LH down RH low)

B and 2 (LH down; RH out)

C and 3 (LH down; RH high)

D and 4 (LH down; RH up - or LH up; RH down)

E and 5 (LH high; RH down)

F and 6 (LH out; RH down)

G and 7 (LH low; RH down)

H and 8 (LH across low; RH

I and 9 (LH across low; RH up)

J and 'alphabetic' (LH out ; RH up)

K and 0 zero (LH up; RH low)

L (LH high; RH low)

M (LH out; RH low)

N (LH low; RH low)

O (LH across high; RH out)

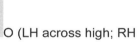
P (LH up; RH out)

123

Q (LH high; RH out)

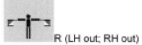

R (LH out; RH out)

S (LH low; RH out)

T (LH up; RH high)

U (LH high; RH high)

V (LH low; RH up)

W (LH out; RH across high)

X (LH low; RH across high)

Y (LH out; RH high)

Z (LH out; RH across low)

Numerical sign (LH high; RH up)

Annul sign (LH low; RH high)

Error (LH and RH raised and lowered together)

124

Meet the Characters

The real Bekka and Ben Cooper...

are Hannah and Ethan Hopewell from Lansing, Michigan.

The real Eli Hartley...

is himself, Eli Hartley from Lansing, Michigan.

Dedication

This book is dedicated to my husband, Randy, who encouraged my telling this story, and to my children, Shannon and Bryon, whose adventures inspired me to write.

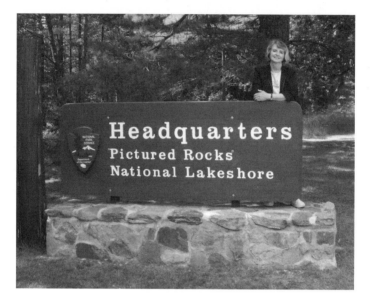

Acknowledgements:

Thank you to...

Randy, my greatest source of encouragement, and Shannon and Bryon, who ate many peanut butter and jelly sandwiches as we traveled thousands of miles to visit America's National Parks.

Maranatha Christian Writers Conference, who bolstered my confidence to pursue this dream.

Richard Baldwin, my publisher, who opened the door, and his staff, who prepared this book for printing.

Shannon, Brenda, Leah, Linda, and Bill for their input.

The children in my life, who became the characters in my book.